Course Correct -
Edited by: Jennifer Miller
Book Formatting: Jennifer Eaton
Cover Designs: DeliciousNightsDesigns.com

To my darling granddaughters –
Stand strong, forever and always.

Chapter One

QUIVINA ADEDEJI

IT'S a funny thing to know you aren't wanted. I wasn't wanted by my husband first. Then, as I stood on the steps of my father's home in Detroit's Boston Edison District, I knew I wasn't wanted there either. He hadn't been my father, not the man I knew growing up, since he learned of my plan to leave my husband two weeks before I landed on his doorstep. Leaving a husband just wasn't something good Nigerian girls did. Never mind that I was forty-five.

"Baba, can you please open the door?" Even as I said the words, I knew he wouldn't.

"Get away from my stoop," he yelled. He used our native Yoruba to prevent the neighbors from understanding us.

"I don't have anywhere else to go," I replied. "It's my house too." My mother had left me money and interest in the house when she died. Of course, if my mother were alive, I wouldn't have been standing on the porch with my face burning more from embarrassment than from the summer sun.

"Quivina, go home to your husband like a good wife. Stop behaving like a whore."

I heard his retreating steps after he dropped the gut punch. The word *asewo* burned over my skin like a brand.

And just like that, our conversation was over. My new job was to start the following week. I was trying to build a new life. The last thing I needed was to be homeless.

"Baba," I called out once more, despite knowing he had turned his back to me even if I couldn't see him through the thick curtains hanging over the door's window.

The silence confirmed what I already knew.

I glanced around at the surrounding oversized Tudor and colonial-style homes and saw curtains falling back into place on more than half. My old neighbors were indeed trolling for details on our argument.

I turned and headed off the porch, down the steps, and back to my Audi, the only thing I'd taken from my marriage. Hadn't I at least earned a car from the deal? For years of abuse, I got a stinking car. Based on my life experience, it was par for the course. I actually hated the parts of it that always seemed to leave me a victim.

Climbing behind the wheel, I reclined my seat and pressed the heels of my palms into my eyes, fighting hard against the latest round of tears. I used the practice tools my therapist had given me. Deep breathing and a look toward the things actually happening and not to those that weren't. Like—my father had refused to allow me into his home, whatever the technicality, but I was not actually homeless. If all else failed, I could stay in a hotel until I found a place. And in reality, perhaps living with my father while he was so pissed at me wouldn't bode well for my mental health.

Just as Dr. Wilson said, life looked a lot better when you

took out the fantasized doom. Also, I had one last card to play. I honestly didn't want to start racking up debt on my credit cards before I started work again.

When I lifted my head, I found several neighbors suddenly walking their dogs. Maybe all of them weren't snooping, but Ms. Oliveras certainly was. I tossed her a wave as she passed my car's bumper, which made her nearly snap her neck turning away.

I hit the start button on my car to let them know the argument was over and I was most likely leaving, then focused on my next move.

I scrolled through the contacts on my phone and found Arnell Strong. She was my oldest and dearest friend. We had gone from undergrad math and science geeks to PhD math and science geeks. From the moment we discovered our similarities, both growing up on the East Side, neither of us being one of the "cool kids," we were practically inseparable. I wish I had met her earlier, back when the high school bullies wouldn't let up on my Nigerian style of dress, or in elementary school when I'd had to train my voice to strip every peak and valley of my pitch so I didn't sound as African as I looked. All in secret, of course, because my parents wholeheartedly believed that it was better to be African than to be African American.

Arnell, or Nell, had become my safe harbor while I was in college, and had remained so until I made the biggest mistake of my life.

"Hey, girl. You touch down yet?" Nell's voice still boomed when she spoke. Heaven help the person who shushed her.

"Nell, hey. I did. Although I drove here since I had so much stuff. I wish I wasn't calling with an ask, though," I said, while trying to keep the embarrassment of being essentially shunned by my father out of my tone.

"Girl, bye. As much as I used your meal plan in college? Stop playing and tell me what's up."

I let out my sigh and remembered why we had always been so close. "My dad won't let me stay here. I think I'll have to sleep on your couch for a few weeks."

"That's it? Of course, you can stay with me. With the promise you'll do the dishes. That is my only rule, take it or leave it."

I had to laugh. Nell had always hated cleaning. "Fine, you have to cook, though."

"Cool, I can do that. When are you coming?"

I squinted my eyes before I told her, even though we weren't on FaceTime. "Today."

"Well, all right. But you do have to finally tell me what all this is about. Why did you up and leave Kenyon, why your dad is tripping... everything. I'm not being nosey," she said, aware of how I felt about opening up when I was embarrassed, "I just think talking will help."

And she was probably right. I hadn't told anyone the full breadth of my situation. "Okay, I think it's time now," I said.

"Seriously, you just made my day." The sound of her shoes against the hardwood came over the receiver, indicating she was doing her trademark shimmy saved for her happiest moments. "I'll text you the address. I should warn you, though, my parking situation is tricky, so be careful with that. I'll let the security guard know you're coming, and he'll let you in. It's going the be just like old times, Q. I can't wait to see you."

"Me, either," I said as I tried to talk around the lump forming in my throat. My voice came out in a hiccup.

"Q, I know doing dishes is the worst, but you don't have to cry about it. I'll do them sometimes, okay?" The smile in her voice was evident, and I appreciated her eternal support.

"See you soon, girl. I need to go get groceries so we don't starve to death. Love you."

"I love you too." Within seconds of hanging up, I received a text with Nell's address on it. I hit the underscored words, then waited for the map to appear on my car's display.

I began to back down Baba's driveway, and as I waited for a car to pass so I could back into the street, I glanced one last time at my father's threshold. The curtain on the door jerked as if someone had pulled it tight. Maybe he would forgive me, eventually.

Just not today.

Chapter Two

MAXWELL WYNN

"I DON'T WANT IT… I don't…" The kid flailed his arms in the universal language of *hell nah*, freezing me in my tracks. "Uncle Max, stop putting it on my plate. I'm not gonna eat it," Donnell scream-explained while I tried my best to feed my nephew. He and his twin sister didn't bother with the formalities of calling me their half-uncle. As far as they were concerned, they were equal-opportunity kids. Donnell and his sister, who fortunately wasn't home at the moment, didn't care about relation, like at all, or whether the whole serving-food-to-kids thing was new to me. Nor were they interested in throwing me a bone on what they *wanted* to eat. Everything was *I don't care* until something was purchased, then presented to them on the table.

I looked down into my nephew's eyes, deep brown orbs that reminded me of my one and only sister—the only person on the planet who could make me think I could take care of kids. The one who was fighting for her life. Her kids had it rough, and there wasn't a second I wasn't aware of the grim unfairness of it all.

Donnell hadn't eaten anything substantial for three days. The boy was down to carrot sticks and hummus. Even I was smart enough to know that wasn't exactly healthy, more like healthy-ish. The last thing I needed was to give Cami one more thing to worry about. He needed protein and a well-balanced meal—according to Slim Goodbody, which was the only relevant reference I could conjure at the moment. So, today's option was pad thai. Apparently, it had been a bad move. A really bad one.

"Donnie, what did we discuss? Having a tantrum isn't the way people communicate. We articulate what we want, or don't want, calmly and with the expectation that the other person will appreciate our rationale."

I stood in place, staring at my family's next generation. Donnie was giving it back to me double time. He didn't look away with the realization he was being unreasonable. It was a game of lunchtime face-off. Who would crack? Would it be hardened veteran, Donnell Jameson, or new-but-nimble Maxwell Wynn? I was ready to take it the full twelve rounds, but I might not have the stamina of my competitor who had been going pound for pound with a military dad and a no-nonsense mother who didn't accept shit from her kids despite loving them down to their dirty socks.

"Uncle Max, would you eat anything that goes against your principles?" Donnell asked, his eyes shifting from wide orbs to narrow slits.

"What exactly is it about Thai food that goes against your principles?" I was just about out of patience but needed to practice what I preached. I was raised to eat what was on the table, a bygone time. The way I was raised was also probably a major reason for my significant trust issues.

"I'm a vegetarian. I told you it when my mom went to the hospital... the second time. When is my dad coming?" Donnie's eyes grew wet with tears. Had to be tough on the kid. With two parents in perilous times, it was enough to break even the hardest-hearted. Nothing about my nephew's heart was hard.

With a sigh, I tried not to let my shoulders sag, placed the spoon into the dish of steaming noodles, and took a seat across the table. "He's deployed. Not gonna lie, I wanted to call him this time too. But your mother doesn't want him to worry. Three months, Donnie. Can you hang with me? I need you to be very strong for your sister... and for your mother." I allowed the deep breath I'd been holding to slip, finally. It was probably one of the hardest conversations I'd had in ages and reminded me of my own childhood... when I realized I would be on my own, so to speak. Except in my case, I'd reacted in a very different way than Donnie.

Donnie blinked a couple of times and crossed his arms as if the thoughts I'd presented had never occurred to him. He would need to be strong. It was a lot for his little shoulders, but I knew he would rise to the challenge. Slouching in his chair, he stared off into the distance for a beat, the act working to crack my heart wide open while watching him. I knew the horrors of watching a mother pass away—to watch as the person responsible for giving life slipped beyond the grasp of human intervention. I prayed the same wasn't happening to my sister, Donnie's mother. Sweet Cami, with her heart of gold.

"I guess I can pick out the chicken," he said, his eyes refocused on me. He didn't smile, and nothing about his expression shifted. But it was probably the best he could do with so much on his mind and in his own heart.

"I'll fish the chunks out for you. And hey—" I stared at

the boy until our eyes met across the table. Donnie finally looked at me with his brows knitted. "I'll never forget you don't eat meat again. Deal?" I meant it. I would not disregard his needs, even if I had to write it on my hand until it sank in. The last thing he needed was someone he relied on to diminish things of significance.

Donnie nodded slowly, his mouth twisted enough to reveal the dimple in his right cheek. Damned if he wasn't Cami's spitting image.

Donnie's twin sister bounded into the room. She was quick and light on her feet, as one would expect from a gymnast. She would have to get to practice soon, and eating a full lunch beforehand wasn't an option for her. She'd had a big breakfast to make up for it. So, instead of grabbing a bowl of carbs along with Donnie, she grabbed the smoothie I'd made to her exact specifications. She needed the fuel, so things like kale, pineapple, and blueberries were thrown in along with a shot of liquid B12. One-point-eight micrograms, to be exact. The specificity was from the coach, and the only way I had remembered it all was by the slip of paper left stuck to the blender.

"Thanks, Uncle Max," she said, not bothering to head to the tiny kitchen table.

I shifted in my seat, turning to watch my niece grab and drink my concoction. "You're welcome, and uh... I put a little honey in it."

"You know I'm not supposed to have it." Diane was a wisp of a girl, smaller than her brother by at least an inch or two. Apparently, sugar—natural or otherwise—wasn't to be had with berries. Our family had a history of diabetes, and Cami wasn't the type to take chances with her kids. Still, I knew exercise burned sugar, so she would be fine. Diane took another sip and gave me a slight smile, her umber skin the same color as her mother's. "It tastes good, though."

"Come sit." I nodded toward the lone empty chair at the triangular-shaped table. "There's at least a half hour before it's time to go. We should... we should um, talk." I had no idea what we were supposed to say, but I knew normal families needed to talk. What one said to two ten-year-old kids when they were processing their mother's illness and a father's deployment simultaneously wasn't in any book I'd ever read... but it still needed to be addressed.

"About what?" Donnie pushed his fork around on the plate to most likely triple-check there weren't any lingering chicken morsels mixed in.

He'd managed to hit my own fears right on the head in just two words. "You guys ready to go back to school?" Yeah, it was a lame question, but it wasn't one of their two biggest issues, so I figured it was safe to start off with something generic.

"Nope," Diane said.

"Why not?" I took a bite of my own food.

"Because we don't have school supplies or new clothes yet." Closing the cap on the travel cup, she shook the smoothie hard and banged the palm of her hand against the bottom.

"Uncle Max can't take us shopping, Di."

"Why not? He has a credit card and money. Mom and Dad would pay him back."

Donnie rolled his eyes. "It's not the money. He doesn't know where to take us. We'd have to go to at least five stores. He can't do it. Maybe Uncle Pronto could, but it's Mom's... thing. She likes to do it."

I held up a finger to interject, even if Donnie was partially correct. I hadn't taken children shopping for school clothes before, but I could google or ask someone where to go, but who, I wasn't sure. But yeah, I could find out. "I can and I will. Right after practice today and when we're done seeing your mom, we're going. There's a few weeks left before school starts, so if we need to make a couple of trips, there's still time to get it all done. End of discussion." The twins looked at me, both skeptical of my use of authoritative tone. "What?" I asked, trying to hide that I'd even managed to amuse myself.

"So... is that your dad voice?" Donnell looked to Di as soon as he said it, a matching set of grins on their faces.

"I'm glad I amuse you, kid. C'mon, let's finish up and head out. Donnie, you've got the dishes."

"Why not Di? She's the girl." Donnie held out both of his hands and made a waving gesture in the air.

I stood and shot Donnie my version of a warning glare. I would not be a contributing factor to Donnie's misogyny. It was perhaps the one thing I knew I could do right as far as the kids were concerned. "That's offensive to your sister. You don't assume women should do domestic tasks any more than we assume all men should eat meat. We all have choices, Donnie. Well, except you, because I told you to put the dishes in the dishwasher. No choice there. Now get to it, bud." I used my finger to direct him toward the sink.

I didn't wait for his response. Instead, I headed to get my shoes and a decent shirt on, but I wasn't too far away to miss Di teasing Donnie about the snap-off. I was still smiling as I made it to my bedroom, grabbing my jacket and car keys after getting dressed. Along the way, my mind flashed back to my sister. She had been moved from the ICU at least, to a telemetry unit. I didn't know much hospital speak, but I assumed that was good.

By the time I returned, wallet and key fob in my pocket, the kids were joking around. The dishes were cleared, takeout container put away, and only a little of the pad thai had made it into the garbage. I had given them a bit of extra alone time. It was important they bond when their family was at such great risk. There was no way to be sure what would happen, and while I prayed for them, I wasn't sure if I should. None of my prayers had been answered in the past so I'd mostly given up.

"Ready?" I asked the twins.

"Yup," Donnie piped up.

Diane remained silent. Her hands were clasped tightly together, shoulders tense and nearly up to her ears.

"Everything okay, baby girl?"

"Well..." She didn't look up. Her eyes were trained on the floor much the same as when she'd broken a bottle of my cologne while practicing a handstand in my bedroom. She had never practiced in front of me and she seemed nervous whenever I brought it up.

I walked over to the table and took the chair closest to her, then turned it toward her and her spot at the island. She was staring at her hands and seemed to be trying to lock her fingers in unnatural positions. "What is it? We share things, right?" It was a play on the words she'd used on me days before when Cami had gone into the hospital unexpectedly. Those kids were too smart for me sometimes.

"It's just that I haven't got the front somersault down. I keep stumbling whenever I land. They're picking the gymnasts for elite status." Her tone and apprehension spoke to how important it was to her. Her words wobbled a bit as she shared what was bothering her, her eyes brimming with unshed tears. Even Donnie stopped adding devices to his backpack for a moment.

"I thought your mom said you have until you were twelve to place. And even then, if you don't make the Olympic squad, there's always college. I know this is important to you, but I don't want you so freaked out that you forget to enjoy yourself." I was serious about that last statement, especially since I'd had more chances than most to see the repercussions of allowing life to pass in a blur while rushing on to the next thing. The *stop and smell the roses* reminder may as well have been on repeat.

"I'm not freaked out at all, and I do enjoy myself. I just want... never mind." Her body language betrayed just about everything she'd said. She rolled her eyes and blew out a long sigh while turning away. Her shoulders slumped as she passed me on the way to the front door.

I had the urge to reach my hands to the heavens, but I was fairly sure the kids didn't want someone who was supposed to look after them to seem helpless. Even if I hadn't asked for spiritual assistance, a plausible response came from the depths of my mind. "Want me to help you practice?"

I didn't even know if that was something Diane was comfortable with, but it seemed like the right thing to do, at least.

Diane stopped walking, and Donnie turned around with his eyes slanted in what I thought was skepticism.

"Uncle Max, you know how to do a forward somersault?" The girl's eyes were wide in amazement.

"No, but I know what they're supposed to look like." I left out the part about dating a gymnast before. Some things shouldn't be shared with kids.

"Right now?" Donnie was less enthusiastic. Understandable. Most kids were impatient as hell, even though they technically had more years than anyone on the planet left. Technically.

"We don't have to be at the gym for a little bit. Only takes me ten minutes to get there. And practice makes perfect, right? Don't you have a yoga mat, Di? We can put it on the front lawn, and you can try a few. Practice always makes me feel better." I was serious about that. I was old-school and believed in my heart that preparation could make all the difference, a belief held in the fabric of my character. Success was merely preparation meeting opportunity, as the saying goes.

A bright smile lit the girl from within, it seemed. "I'll get it," she said before practically hopping off down the hall to the bedroom. My neighbors would probably hate me by the time the children left, but if I could make their lives better for just a moment, I would.

It didn't take us much time at all with little Di urging us on. We were down the hall, down the stairs, and on the front lawn of my apartment complex in a matter of minutes. I helped her roll out the mat and positioned Donnie on one end to help her if she needed it to get started, then stood at the other end of the mat to catch her if she couldn't stop.

Things went well. Diane nailed first the double. Then a single with a twist. Her smile was bright and wide as confidence grew within her. It was as if I could see it radiating from her. After about ten minutes, we were ready to go, and if I hurried, I would get her there on time and catch Cami right after her testing ended for the day. I wanted to have at least Donnie there to greet her. Cami had insisted Di go on to her practice, as always, to give them some semblance of a routine despite her illness.

Rounding the corner to the parking lot, I came to a halt. "Dammit..." I tried to curse under my breath. Cami rarely cursed, and I was trying to live up to her impossible perfection while I had her kids.

But the scene before me warranted the word, with a *fuck me* thrown in for good measure. The back parking lot was narrow. The entrance and exit were essentially one narrow lane and drivers had to be especially considerate with their cars. This one wasn't.

Behind my Wrangler was a shiny black Audi, parked at an angle with the trunk open. Undoubtedly, the owner would be back soon. "All right kids, go ahead and get in the car. Looks like we'll be delayed just a bit."

"Okay. I can be a few minutes late, Uncle Max," Di said as she headed to the car, Donnie right behind her.

I popped the locks with my key fob and considered taking the doors off since it was such a nice day and I had newly found time since some jackass had blocked me in. I opted for the front doors. I wasn't brave enough to have the kids riding with me without the back doors. Since they rode in the back, they would be safe, and I would get to enjoy what was bound to be one of the last hot summer days the way a Jeep owner should. Without doors. "While we wait, I'm taking these doors off."

"Yay," Donnie yelled. "Shotgun." His arms were in the air, and he went for the front seat.

"Nope. In the back, sir. I've known my sister longer than you and she'll kill me if you come in looking like all your dreams came true. Women can sniff out when you're having a good time. You'll find out about that when you're older." I let out a knowing laugh as Donnie and Di looked at me quizzically.

"It's just a little ways," he said, the frown on his face quickly replacing the smile.

"Nope. In the back. No arguing. If you're cool with this, we can go to Cold Stone on the way home. Deal?"

"Me too," Di chimed in.

"Oh yeah. You do like ice cream, don't you?" I teased.

"You know it's my favorite." She rolled her eyes before climbing into the back seat.

"I forgot. Sue me," I said with a wink to my niece. I made quick work of getting the doors off and placing them in the storage unit. But it was another five minutes before the owner of the car showed up. And oh man... did she know how to make an entrance.

The woman walking to the open trunk was tall. Nearly as tall as me, but she was wearing heels. A red sundress flowed behind her, revealing a sumptuous physique. Her body was that of a goddess. On any other day, I would have had something else on my mind altogether. But not today.

I walked over to her, clearing my throat. She smelled of fresh-cut flowers. "Excuse me, Miss?"

When I reached her, I saw her hand on the handle of the luggage piece with it halfway out of the car. As festive as everything was, from her curly mane of wild hair blowing in the breeze as if on purpose, to the red and green high-heeled sandals covering her feet, the look on her beautiful face betrayed all of it. She looked upset, and if I would have delved a bit more, hurt was evident. But I didn't have time for all that. Family obligations took precedence over everything, even gorgeous women who had lips made for kissing.

"Yes," she responded sharply with a voice clipped in African accent. Southern corner, maybe? Her brows were tight and mouth pressed into a thin line. It was as if waves of frustration rolled from her. I had the urge to massage her bare, deep brown shoulders, just to coax the muscles that were sure to be knotted with tension. This woman probably had no poker face to speak of, because I could see sadness in her chocolate-hued eyes.

For a moment, I was lost in trying to figure her out, but given the circumstances, I had to push away the stuff that was none of my business and get back to what was most pertinent at the time. She was blocking my car in, and now my niece would be late and Cami wouldn't find Donnie waiting in the hospital room when she returned. None of that was this mystery woman's fault, but ignoring the posted signs to not block neighbors in their spot was definitely her issue.

"Sorry to bother you," I said, once my mouth started working again. "I'm in a bit of a hurry. Do you think you could move your car so that I can get out?"

"Oh," she said, the tension in her face easing just a bit. "Yes, I can. I just have one more bag and then I can—"

"No, ma'am. You see, I have somewhere to be in a few minutes I'm actually already late. If you don't mind... I can help you with your bag while you move forward if you like..." I allowed my words to trail off, hoping she picked up on the restrained calmness I attempted.

"Yeah, I get that. I'll just be a moment..."

"I don't have minutes. Like I said, I can give you a hand."

I don't usually notice folks emoting in my direction—a hazard of being a professor to freshmen, but I distinctly noted her rolling her eyes at me.

"No, I have it. Don't worry about it." Then, as if I were the cause of the problem, she sighed. She was cute but obviously some kind of prima donna. The fact that I didn't have time for women lately, much less the kind who didn't know how rude it was to block someone in, drove away any thoughts of trying to get this smoking-hot lady's telephone number.

Too late, anyway. She was already around the car and in the driver's seat before I could say another damn word.

Fine then, be that way. I was obviously angry about being blocked in, but maybe more so, she annoyed me with her seeming lack of regard.

I glanced down at my watch and noted the time. I would have to go right then if I didn't want Di to be charged an extra fifty bucks for being over a half hour late. Her coach called it a "respect" fee, and it went to pay for team extras.

While it made sense and was part of the rules, I still didn't want my sister saddled with an extra bill. Even though I would pay it, unnecessary stress for Cami wouldn't do. Pushing thoughts of this mystery woman and probably the first woman I'd been attracted to in at least a year aside, I climbed into the driver's seat scented with my nephew's spray-can, drugstore body spray and put the car into reverse the moment the black Audi was far enough away for me to ease by it without taking any of her paint.

Crisis averted, I backed out of the slot and ignored the woman who had pulled her car ahead, nearly touching the wrought-iron fence and barricade to the dumpster. No matter how well-maintained the condo's exterior landscape was, the garbage cans would have a smell. As much as that shouldn't have been my business, I pulled out and blew the horn to get her attention. She'd already gotten out of her car, but she didn't have the trunk open again. I rolled down the window and leaned my head out to tell her, "Hey, you can use my spot to unload." I pointed to the space I'd just left.

The woman didn't say anything but gave a slight nod and tossed a wave in acknowledgment of my statement. She didn't smile either. Instead, she ran the palm of her hand over her face as she turned around to get back in the car. Damned if something inside me didn't yearn for it—I wanted that smile.

I also wanted to help her with her bags. Even if I was perturbed by her blocking me in, none of that dissuaded me from being a gentleman. She had not allowed me to, which was another thing that niggled in the back of my mind. Why not?

Just as well, right? I reminded myself of my other, more important obligations and that there was precious little time to take care of Cami and watch out for the twins. And then there was Smith, my younger brother who needed me, even if he didn't want to admit it. Yup, there was too much. My life was a mess. No need to drag anyone else into the muck.

As I pulled away with one more glance in my rearview mirror at the striking, ebony-skinned beauty, wavy tresses blowing in the wind, I wondered, even if briefly, whether there would ever be time again.

Chapter Three

NELL EMBRACED me so hard my breath escaped. I sank into the arms of my best friend, sorority sister, and confidante. I had been away for a few years, yet it still felt like home. Enveloped in her familiar Clinique-scented embrace, I was thankful she still loved taking care of people.

"It's been far too long. God, I've missed you." Nell released me a little, still holding my shoulders, and looked me over once, then again as if she no longer recognized me. It had been too long since I'd seen her in person. "God, Q. I'll hug on you all day if I don't stop myself." She was one of the only people close to me who called me Q. "How are you doing?"

"Yeah... it's been way too long. I won't let that happen again," I whispered into her long, curly red hair before stepping away. Arnell hadn't changed in the slightest bit. Her warm brown skin was still velvet soft, and her eyes reminded people of the sweetest Manuka honey. She was beautiful, always had been. The quintessential African American beauty queen. So very unlike me, but my adopted sister, nonetheless. "And I'm fine. After I was confronted by some tall, fine-ass dude. I think he was going to call the police. Girl, your neighbors are hardcore."

Nell rolled her eyes and waved her slender fingers in the air in dismissal of my concerns. "That could have been a hundred different people. Some of the neighbors are kind of cute, but definitely pains in the ass. Get your butt in here." She leaned in to pick up one of my luggage pieces and waved me in. She turned around and walked into the huge condo. Once a warehouse, it was newly converted with windows so wide, I could already see her view from the door. Her orange-scented incense spilled into the hallway, and I didn't even need to step in to smell the undercurrent of burned white sage. Arnell had always been a believer in the power of herbs and crystals.

I grabbed the remaining two bags and followed her in, still a bit winded from the two trips I'd needed to make up and down the stairs. "Thank you for letting me stay here. I don't know what I would have done. I didn't expect Baba to react that way, honestly."

I hadn't. I thought he was just complaining because of the divorce. I thought he was just angry at the situation and would surely understand my position, given what he'd said during the phone call, since it was *my* decision. He'd been controlling me since the start, and now he was withholding even shelter. A man who would do something like that to his only child... his only remaining family in the States... well, he wasn't even remotely similar to the man I'd known my entire life, after all.

"Don't you say it again. You are my sister. Whatever I have is yours. Except my vibrator. Please don't borrow that." Nell had always had a darker sense of humor.

"Gross."

"Yeah, yeah... well, this is it." She led me into a wide-open space with colorful walls in red and green, sage furniture, an array of decorative pillows in Indian motif, and African statues from every country she'd visited on the continent. Not a single item in her living room was surprising. When we were kids, my father and mother had let her come home to Nigeria with us for the summer, and she had been fascinated with everything about Africa ever since. Her trips were frequent and always ended with lots of newfound art, clothes, and an even deeper interest in her own lost ancestry.

"Oh Nell, your décor is stunning." I set my luggage in the corner of the room near the wall-to-wall windows, then took a seat on the ledge. The view faced downtown from her Midtown Detroit condo and was wholly breathtaking. It almost made walking up six flights of stairs worth it.

"Thank you. My mom calls it Bohemian, which is also her term for lesbian... which she'd never admit." Wry laughter capped off her cynicism.

"You should tell her you're pansexual, not a lesbian. It'll take her a month to figure it out." I offered a sympathetic smile.

"Whatever. Not my job to educate. I have enough problems. Which we aren't talking about, by the way." Nell took a seat on the floor and grabbed a pillow on her lap. "What are we eating? And more importantly, what are we drinking? I wanted to find out how your father reacted before deciding what to cook. I didn't know what the carb count should be."

A giggle escaped me, even if the confrontation between my father and me had been nothing less than explosive. I leisurely lifted the window, letting in some air to distract myself. The scent of lilacs outside drifted in on the soft breeze. "I'd say macaroni and cheese-level carbs."

"Oh shit... like epically bad? We're talking def-con twelve?"

"Nuclear. But you know what?" I turned to face her despite the pit of embarrassment churning in my stomach.

"Hmm..."

"I don't regret my choices." I felt the tears burning from the corners of my eyes. My heart clenched at the thought of all the pain I'd been through, but I had taken it. I had rejected the alimony from my ex with the exception of my car, my father's demands that I forgive and forget, and finally, living a life completely dedicated to someone else's ideal. For all the extra pain it caused, it was worth it. "I'll get by on my own."

"Damn right, you will. Tequila and tacos, I think. Yes?"

I turned back to my friend, her gently upturned lips offering the same unwavering support and love as when we'd pulled all-nighters in college and decided on one inappropriate breakfast or another before heading off to class. "I think that works, Nell. You've never let me down, my friend."

"Never will, chick. Now, I'll be right back. I've got Patrón in the fridge, and I need to grab the menu for Alley Taco. I didn't buy anything to make tacos. This restaurant wasn't here when you last visited, but trust me, it's the bomb." Nell got to her feet and adjusted the cut-off jogging pants and midriff-exposing top she sported. Even though we were over forty, she still dressed like we had in college. Well, around the house she did, I imagined. Can't be a physics professor for a major institution and show up looking like a teenager.

I envied her boldness though. Where Nell had taken her time in her late twenties and early thirties to figure out who she was, I had used that time to build what I thought was a home for my husband. What would have been a home for our children.

Looking back, it was a good thing everything hadn't gone as planned because if we'd had kids, there would be other lives starting over and not just mine. Thank goodness for small blessings, I guess. "I'm sure it's great," I called after her.

I turned my face back to the window and looked down into the parking lot instead of over the horizon. I had left my car double-parked because along with gentrification came extremely shitty parking. Nell had warned me, but nothing could have prepared me for the endless block-circling that came with Midtown. I had not been prepared for the aggressive drivers either. They were like piranhas, waiting for the next juicy morsel to drop before swarming it with their tiny Priuses and Smart Cars. Long gone were the days of parking anywhere near campus and not being added to a six-month waiting list for an overpriced studio apartment. But it was what it was. I had expected to live with my father then move into my own place once it became available. It wasn't fair to call Nell with my shit, especially since I hadn't exactly been close to her in the last decade and a half. I had reached out to tell her about the divorce and when I would move back home. True to form, Nell hadn't judged or asked questions. She'd just let me share what I wanted to, stopping to offer consolation when I stopped speaking and cried in spells.

"All right, I want you to take a look at this menu right after you take this shot," she said, walking across the room to hand me a glass so cold, there were fingerprints in the light frost from the chilled liquid.

"I don't know if I'm ready for a sh—"

"Drink it," she snapped, licking the salt from her hand and holding onto the lemon as she tipped her head back and downed the contents of her glass. "Ummph, that was good." Even if her face was twisted into a grimace and she was rubbing her chest.

With appraising eyes, she looked me up and down. "What?"

I wasn't ready for the burn. It had been a long time since I drank anything. Kenyon wasn't a fan of drinking, controlling ass that he was, which meant I couldn't be a fan of drinking.

"You're still holding that glass of tequila."

"I was just letting it warm up a bit," I said, before staring down into the deep shot glass.

"Drink, girl. You used to love this stuff."

I didn't bother to argue about us leaving behind all the things that came with college life once we had PhDs in hand. In Nell's case, she went about building a career, became a tenured professor, wrote works beyond the dissertations we'd both had to submit. Meanwhile, I was building a life as the wife of a physician—married to a top-ranking surgeon who dragged us from Atlanta to San Diego, Denver, and finally back to Atlanta before he'd picked up a mistress. All I did in that time was throw dinner parties.

I took the shot. In addition to the minuscule shards of ice chilling my teeth as it passed to my throat, it burned going down, as if I'd swallowed pure fire. The strong aftertaste of alcohol chased the flames into my stomach. "Wow, that is potent. Was it always that strong?" I asked, my hand going to my chest to rub out the fire instinctively and as if I was mimicking Nell.

"That means it's good. I just ordered a smorgasbord of tacos. What's the movie of the night?" she asked.

I rolled the shot glass between my fingers as I pondered the question. It had been a long time since I'd considered... well, anything purely for my own enjoyment. My entire existence had been made up of whatever task, project, or action would make the people around me happy. Even making the choice of a movie to watch felt wonderful. Such a simple thing could have an impact, and I briefly struggled to find a single moment in the past decade where I'd done something solely for me. "Do you know that Netflix ghost movie? It was a holiday mov—"

"Do I know it? It's the one with the appraiser who had to decide if having the best sex of her life for ten days out of every year was enough to last her the rest of her years? I should own stock in that damn movie." Nell leaned back into the couch, face twisted as she swallowed her own shot. She was my non-judgey friend who would watch cheesy holiday movies in late July with no questions asked.

"I mean, it's epically perverse, but I loved it. We could watch that, I guess."

"Yes, because sis was ready to risk it all for some ghostly D. Come on, have a seat on the couch." She got to her feet. "I'm going to get my television."

"You gave up that mounted monster?" I asked, doing as she requested and plopping onto her incredibly soft couch in a heap.

"No, no. I still have the one in my bedroom. I will never take it down. This one is my kitchen TV. And while we look for the movie, I have something to tell you." Nell wriggled her eyebrows the way she did whenever she had something up her sleeve. Perhaps I should have been nervous about Nell's unspoken plans, but she knew I was in a vulnerable state. It was bound to be something harmless.

"Okay... but do you have something a little weaker to drink? I'm afraid my liver isn't up to the test. I need to ease into being a party girl again."

"Fine, but you're kind of being weak as balls."

"Never..." Sitting up straight, I stuck my chin out in a

display of strength, even if we both knew how very fragile I was.

By the time we finished the first bottle of wine, I was more relaxed, and the couple from the movie was discovering they could not live without one another... even if the dude was a ghost. But Nell still hadn't shared what she wanted to tell me.

"All right, Nell. What's up?" Though I wasn't sure I was ready for what Nell had in store for me, all I could hope was that it wasn't anything that would require any amount of energy on my part. I was exhausted from the ordeal with my father and honestly wanted to put the entire day behind me.

"I'm waiting for the right moment."

"Spit it out," I demanded.

"I signed you up for One Cupid." The statement came out in a rush, and instantly, I knew exactly why she'd beat around the bush before telling me.

I was on the verge of blowing up but somehow managed to hold the outburst. "You did what, now?"

"I signed you up to see if you can find someone to date again. I figured you'd need to get your swagger back."

"Oh, Nell. That was... not a good idea." I knew she meant well, but it was pretty presumptive on her part.

"Why not? You aren't looking for a husband. Just someone to have fun with."

"What if I don't like the guys—I mean, what if they don't like me? It's not as if I'm super hot and attractive... I'm almost an old lady." A forty-five-year-old woman wasn't exactly what most men were looking for on dating apps, from what I'd heard.

I grew more and more nervous as she opened the app and began to swipe over face after face, each one more attractive than the last.

"Stop being a wimp, Quivina. You don't have anything

to lose by going out with one of these dudes. Just think of it like an adventure. Each date is merely meant to be a fun experience, no strings, no commitments. Just fun times with some randoms you don't have to see again if you don't want to."

"I'm just not sure I'm confident enough." My pulse raced with each sentence she uttered. "I'm very nervous about this. I don't know how else to explain that to you."

Nell sighed, loud and exasperated. "Just try it. Just give it a try and I promise I'll leave you alone. Deal? If you hate it, we'll delete your profile together immediately. They don't even have your real name. No one will ever be able to tie you back to it. Anyway, it's just like riding a bike. You get back up on that dick, plop down on it, then you pedal as fast as you can." As she explained the very dirty analogy, she reared back, feet in the air, and made a pedaling motion.

"I'm pretty sure that's not how this all works."

"How would you know? You haven't been out there for years. Hell, decades."

"Oh, shut up. But you are my girl and I trust you implicitly. I just don't know if anyone here piques my interest. If I find someone, I'll reach out to him. If... *when* it doesn't work, I'm gonna leave this alone and so will you. That's the deal, right?"

"Fine, but you know I am a firm believer that you should always take the bull by the horns or the dick by the balls... You never know what's out there if you don't look."

"You are so gross, Nell." Raising my hand to my mouth, I pretended to gag myself before taking the phone from her. During my scroll, I realized how very out of touch I was on the dating scene. Everybody seemed so superficial. I wasn't sure how faces could appear vain and shallow just on their own, but they did.

It just wasn't for me. No way was I going to find a

person I'd like… Then, I saw someone who didn't look quite the same as everyone else. His smile was genuine and it reached his eyes. He had a nut-brown skin color—a warm, cocoa-butter shade. He was gorgeous, and his warmth reached from the phone and touched me.

I hadn't seen that in the app at all. There was nothing in those nameless men that made me want to be with any of them, except this guy. I hadn't wanted to be with anyone since I had left Kenyon. And even as I looked at this stranger on Nell's phone screen, considering whether to swipe right or swipe left, I thought back to the guy in the parking lot.

Even though he was angry with me for blocking his car, he'd made me feel something, some gentle stirring deep inside me. I certainly wouldn't turn him down if he turned up on the app.

Whatever—he wasn't going to be on there, and I needed to quit stalling.

That's it… I would just pick someone and maybe I'd have some fun for a change… Maybe the guy wouldn't be a weirdo…. Maybe I should stop being *weak as balls*, and be like every other young woman in the world. If I had done that when I was younger, perhaps I wouldn't have missed my youth and married someone who'd never really even cared about me.

I took my wine and plopped down on the couch next to Nell and looked at her. "All right, that's fine. I'm going to go through with this. I'll pick one of these poor wretches, and I'll go out with them… Does that suit you? And I want to update my profile pic. You picked one from years ago. I look like a kid." He actually wasn't a poor wretch at all, but my pic looked like a throwback to my college days. My hair was curled in one of those Aunt Viv styles.

Nell took the phone from me and smiled approvingly. "Yup, it actually does look pretty old-school. Beggars can't be choosers. And I pulled that picture from Facebook. I presumed you liked it. I'll find another. Now, you go change into something that isn't so Sally-going-to-market looking…"

"There is nothing wrong with my clothes."

"You look like a colorful Amish person."

"Says you, you trite witch. I like the way I dress, and I will not be changing my attire for some dude I don't know. He needs to see me in all my cheerful glory."

Nell and I giggled for the rest of the night. We watched more old movies, and for the first time in a long time, I felt like I had someone in my corner who really cared about me. It was better than a date. Frankly, it was better than anything because my friend was there for me. Even if she hated my clothes and even if she hated the fact that I hadn't been on a date since I left Kenyon, she would follow me and be in my corner. Exactly as she should be.

And that was what I needed more than anything—at least for that night.

Chapter Four

QUIVINA

"**THERE IS** something you can help with... And I really, really, really need you to be open-minded. I've been thinking about it for a while," I started pensively. It was four in the morning, and we had gone back to the tequila.

"Anything, girl. You know I gotcha back."

"Well, I think... I think I want to go natural."

"What? You going natural finally?" Nell sat up, a wide smile growing over her face.

"Yes, bitch." I rolled my eyes. "I do want to go natural, always have. I just never did because Kenyon said it wasn't appropriate for a doctor's wife to walk around with *her nappy hair all over the place.*"

"You would think that son of a bitch would be a bit more enlightened than that. You guys did live in Atlanta for all those years."

"Yeah, tell me about it. Anyway, now that I'm on my own and starting over again, I think it's the perfect time. It will be something that represents me, you know what I mean? I want to be the person I always imagined I would be before I married some dude my father picked for me and gave my life away. You know, by now I thought I would be somebody great. I thought I would've discovered a new theory or cured cancer... Hell, I don't know. I would've done something..."

"I'm pretty sure you can't cure cancer with physics, but I get what you mean." Nell nudged me gently in the ribs to let me know she was joking. "It's like trying to track down what would have happened if you hadn't stepped on the wrong path."

"Right? I just want to see who I am. I spent my whole life being something and everything for someone else. If it wasn't my father, it was Kenyan, and I've never had the chance to figure it out on my own."

"I know, but none of us knew who we were and what we wanted from day one. Most of us grew up living by someone else's beauty standards. Someone else's thoughts for who we should become. We were never given an opportunity just to stand there with our eyes wide open, daring to believe."

"I guess that's what I'm saying. I guess I want to take the time to figure this out. Does that sound crazy? At my age..."

"No, girl. Sounds a lot like bravery." Nell stood up and extended the champagne flute she'd been using to drink the white wine in my direction, touching it to the lip of my glass. "Here's to becoming who the fuck we should be." The clinking sounded out into the night air while Love Jones played on in near silence in the background.

"Cheers."

Another two or three hours later, we were standing in her bathroom looking at a woman I didn't even recognize.

"Whose goddamn hair is that?"

"That's how everybody's hair looks, girl. In the beginning."

Nell's positive, reassuring face stared back at me in the mirror. I could see she wanted me to believe in myself as much as she did. Of course she believed in me—that's what best friends did, especially when they went as far back as we did.

"I guess I just... I didn't expect it to look so sparse. I mean, I used to have beautiful hair."

"It still is, it's just used to being straight. So, instead of curling up, it does... that." Nell pointed at the stringy ends extending from my semi-curled hair halfway up each strand. "That's what years of bad perms and over-processing leave behind. But give it time—when you're ready to cut off all those dead ends, your hair will look like it did before. That's what we're doing after all, right? You're starting over from where you should've been all along?"

I looked back at my own reflection, trying to understand what she was saying to me. I looked for the girl who used to stay up all night and make espressos with her best friend. I looked for the girl who used to have confidence, who knew what she wanted to be in life and all the things she needed to do. I looked for the girl I once was before it was all stolen away from me.

After another few minutes, I began to see her. "All right. Let's cut it."

"Okay when you say cut it, you mean trim it? Or do you mean cut it? Because once I make the first cut, we can't go back. Like... no way can you go back. You'll be at square one. There are other options. We could transition—" Nell picked up her phone, no doubt to start scrolling through throngs of YouTube vids showing the wide and varying options.

"No." I didn't want the coward's way out. I wanted to

be as brave as I was trying to make myself believe I was. I wanted to start again. And I guess that meant I wanted to be new from the roots of my hair to the balls of my feet.

There is a Bible verse, talks about rejuvenation. It speaks to pouring new wine into old wineskins, and I think that's where I was. I would need to pour my new self into a fresh wineskin if I wanted positive results. That's what I wanted, to be new. And I wouldn't get that being afraid. "Yeah, let's cut it. It's what I want. And if you don't do it, I'll just go get someone else."

"All right, girl, I just wanted to be sure you know what you're getting into. I'm down with whatever. And if you want to start fresh with a petite, teeny-weeny Afro, then that's what the hell we're doing today."

As brave as I was pretending to be, I couldn't watch as Nell cut strands from my hair and piles of it landed on the floor. My eyes were closed, with me peeking at the growing stack every few minutes. My heart danced in my chest, and my breath came in short bursts. I was afraid of who I was going to see when I opened my eyes and looked in the mirror again. I hadn't even imagined I would make it that far.

"All right Quivina. I'm all done. You can open your eyes."

And so I did. Not gonna lie, it wasn't anything I'd expected. Everything about my face was different than I'd imagined. My forehead looked larger, my eyes looked wider set, and my mouth seemed like the lips were so full, they didn't even belong to me. My cheekbones jutted out, and my nose was far less prominent in comparison to all of it. "This isn't what I expected."

"It never is. But you know what we do now?"

"What?"

"We start the work." Nell leaned down and gave me a

kiss on the cheek, then she wrapped her warm arms around my neck and pulled me close to her chest, like a mother would do when her daughter was sad.

While I hadn't even known it, it was the thing that I needed most in the world in that moment. I clutched my hands around her forearms as if I were trying to keep from floating away.

"Thank you." My voice cracked on the words. I could barely get them out. I was more thankful than I ever knew I would be.

I looked back at myself in the mirror then. The girl that I saw was so very different than I remembered. It was like looking at a warrior. Those full lips, wide-set eyes, forehead —all of it was so very proud. For the first time, I realized that girl in the mirror was who I should have been the entire time.

Chapter Five

MAX

I TOOK a look around the cold hospital room. While I knew why we were there, and that all these machines helped people, it wasn't the place for my sister. My sister, Cami, was a sweetheart who was always there for everyone else. Her spirit and her soul were bright beacons of light for everyone she encountered. She should not have been lying in a hospital bed.

I really wanted to help her, more than anything I'd ever wanted. But she had a rare illness that caused her organs to attack one another. The damn thing was called Goodpasture Syndrome, as if there were anything good about it, and I'd never even heard of it before the day she told me about the diagnosis. Initially, the doctors had thought it was a virus. The worst part was waiting to find out what could have been ravaging her in such a fast-moving and aggressive way.

It shouldn't have been her. So many people that I knew and loved had been taken, and I wasn't ready to let her go. The familiar nip of guilt sank its teeth into my heart. Cami had everything to live for, and me... well, I was dispensable. She had kids and a life, while I wouldn't be missed.

She wasn't in the room when we arrived, though. I was too late. I was supposed to be there with Donnie before she went off for her next round of tests. My sister had entrusted me with her children, and she wasn't one of the people that I needed to let down. She'd been there for me through all of my shit, the ups and downs I'd taken the family through. Cami was the type of woman who deserved everything, and I couldn't even manage her kids' schedules.

"Uncle Max, do you know when she'll be back?" Donnie placed his backpack on the floor, then sat on the windowsill of the hospital room, his feet dangling as he waited for a response.

"No... I don't know, but it should be soon. You know she won't stand for them keeping her away from you too long." I smiled, though it was the last thing I felt like doing. I needed to keep on a brave face for him though.

"But I want to show her what I made her." Donnie reached into his pack, then held up a drawing. It was the likeness of his mother, the planes of her face so lifelike in the pencil sketch that it made me want to weep.

"Damn," I whispered, "looks just like her."

"Well... duh, that's what it's supposed to look like." He rolled his eyes and let out a little chuckle.

He was the jokester of my little sister's family, after all. He was the one who reminded me that life wasn't so serious all the time and probably the only one in the family who didn't take everything to heart. Donnie smiled more than he was upset, making a point to remember that life is for living. Even at his young age, I knew he was going to grow up to be a great person. "I know, I know. I'm just saying, it's better than I expected. You might make a great artist one day."

"One day? I'm a great artist now, Uncle Max." He rolled

the paper between his hands into a cylinder. Before I could stop him, he leaned over and rapped me on the knuckles with it.

"I don't have to remind you about having confidence, huh?"

"I've got confidence to spare. That's what Mommy says, anyway," he said.

Putting on a display of strength even when it was the furthest thing from reality must have been hereditary. I knew neither of us felt any semblance of ease or comfort, yet there we were... pretending to be okay for one another.

I remembered when I had been in a very similar hospital room watching my own mother. When she left me, it seemed like the whole world was going to open wide and swallow me whole. It didn't even take two weeks before I was living with my father, someone I hardly knew, with a brand-new family. Smith and Cami became my siblings, but I never forgot the cozy comfort of my life with my mother before she passed away. And as much as my father's wife, Evelyn, tried to make me feel at home, it was missing something so dear to me. Back then, I couldn't put my finger on it.

So I knew how Donnie felt—no matter how much I tried to make his and Diane's life similar if not the same as living with his mother, it would never measure up to life with her. If it came down to that...

"Your mother is a smart woman," I said.

The words kind of just hung there in the expanse of the hospital room, missing the bed. Silence enveloped us, and Donnie and I didn't say anything for a long time. Even as he slid from the windowsill to go slump in the chair across the room.

The doctors and nurses carried on outside the room while we waited for what felt like an eternity for my sister, his mother, to return from her midday tests. They should take as long as they needed though. The medical staff was trying to get a handle on her disease. It was one that was as complex as it was mysterious, and as hard as they tried, they seemed to keep coming away with more and more questions. I wanted so desperately for one of the many, many doctors to come in and tell me that everything was going to be okay. But somehow in my heart, I knew it wouldn't wrap up so simply. I knew that her illness was something that they didn't even know how to handle, at least not in our small part of the world. Detroit had a great many things, but apparently the solution to curing this disease was not one of them.

Eventually, we did hear the sound of her gurney being pushed over the floor. Donnie's head popped up just in time for him to see his mother as they wheeled her into the room. A great, wide smile spread across his small, cherubic face.

"Mommy," he said, standing from his chair.

Even though she must've been dog-tired, my sister forced a smile on her face. "Hey, sweetheart," she said, the weakness of her eyes betraying the broad smile on her face, "I'm so sorry it took me so long."

"It wasn't that long, Cami," I said. "We just got here a little bit ago. It took us forever to get out of the house. Your kids nearly killed me because I'm apparently incapable of making a solid meal." I laughed. I wanted to lighten the mood. I didn't want her to worry about her kids—it was the last thing that she needed to be concerned with. I wanted her to focus on getting well. I needed her to be 100% for those kids. They didn't deserve the hand that they'd been dealt. Their father was in the Marines and deployed. The kids didn't even know Cami and Donald weren't together. They'd been waiting until he was back home to tell them. Then Cami got sick, and even though we knew nothing would ever be the same again, we all pretended, nevertheless.

"I'm pretty sure you're telling me a story, Max," Cami said. "But that's okay. I'm coming to expect that." She gave me a warm smile, fully aware that I was full of shit.

"Mommy, I made you something." Donnie rushed over to the bed as soon as the orderlies got her into position and the wheels locked in place. He unrolled the picture slowly, his hands careful not to tear any of the paper, and held it vertically so she could see the full expanse of the picture. I watched as her eyes lit with pride and love, and probably the most important thing, motherly understanding of what it all meant. She knew that Donnie was trying to remember her. He was trying to create something beyond the images in his mind to remind him of his mother if she were to happen to leave him.

I knew that well because I had made some pictures of my own mother in her final days. The bitter truth of it had been that one day my mother wouldn't be there anymore. And no matter how hard that had been to accept as a child, I had to. So I did. The only part that had been up for question was when.

I watched those kids every day, hoping they wouldn't have to go through what I had. That they would grow into adults and have kids of their own before they had to face the ultimate finality of every human's life and our own mortality. I didn't want them to go through the pain of wondering why their mother had been taken. I spent all my teenage years in that very constant battle.

While ultimately my choices were meant to be self-destructive, I had destroyed so many lives in the process of coming to my own resolution. And now, as an adult standing in my sister's room, I was really trying to make amends. I needed to make good on all the things that I had taken away from so many of the people that I loved. I caused the accident that ruined Smith's life. I had taken away our father in one foolish act. And unlike most murderers, I never had to pay with jail time. It wasn't even considered manslaughter. The accident I had caused was ruled to be just that—an accident. That day over two decades ago, I'd wanted the police to tell me that I was wrong. I wanted them to punish me for everything that I had done. But they didn't, and I never felt any resolution for the damage that I had caused.

So, I spent the years trying to make it up to both Smith and Cami. And while I was watching my sister fight for her life, I never felt like it would ever, ever be enough.

"Oh my goodness. This is beautiful. Thank you, my darling." Cami's eyes welled with tears.

"I was trying to get it just right. I was trying really hard, but your eyes... you see," Donnie said, tracing his hands over the picture, "they're really hard to do. They don't look like they used to, and when I try to draw them I can never remember how they were."

My sister grabbed a tissue off the table that was beside her bed and dabbed at tears that she was trying so desperately to hold inside. "No, son. It is perfect. I love it. And... I love you." Cami reached out her hands for her son. He looked up to her and moved forward, crushing the picture between them as she folded him into her, his little body hanging half off the bed.

Like so many times throughout my life, I felt like an interloper. I felt like I didn't belong there. I looked down at the floor to keep from observing something so intimate and so special.

I'd never truly felt like I belonged in the family. I never felt like I was part of them. It was like I was an onlooker, a stranger they were just too kind to turn away. "I uh... I'll be back in a few minutes. I have a few calls to make and some emails to check before I go back to work. Donnie, take all the time you need. I'll be back to get you soon," I said as I left the room.

"Okay," Cami said behind me.

I did not stop to look back at my sister. I didn't stop in the hallway, nor look up as I passed the people at the nurse's station, or anyone in the sterile, brightly lit hallways. That way, I didn't have to make the small talk necessary to let them know that I was okay and that I wouldn't break under the pressure. Instead, I brushed past them and headed straight for the elevator, hit the down button, and shoved my hands deep into my pockets. I prayed the doors opened quickly so that I wouldn't collapse under the weight of my guilt and sadness right there in the hallway.

The doors opened and I stepped aside, allowing the occupants off the elevator. They were barely past me when I jumped inside and moved to the back of the carriage. The doors closed, and it was then and only then that I pressed my hands into my locs in an effort to keep my head on straight. Inside the safety of the elevator, I prayed that I would have the ability to take care of those kids until Cami's ex-husband got home from the Marines if she didn't... I didn't even want to think the words.

Smith wasn't in any condition to take care of them—he was dealing with his amputation. There were still times when he needed revision surgeries. And even though his life was going better after receiving the position of assistant coach for the Southeast Michigan University Cavaliers, he still had struggles that he would never be done with. There were so many things I wanted for him—to meet someone, to fall in love and have his own children one day. Even if it sometimes seemed he would never have time for those things given he only focused on his career, I still wanted it for him. I wasn't going to saddle him with two kids when he had so much shit on his plate.

I'd never found someone I cared enough about. I knew that even when I'd gotten married, so the divorce didn't come as a surprise. I had only been half a man for the whole of our relationship. It wasn't Marilyn's fault. And as unfair as it was for me to marry her in the first place, I had just needed something to hold on to. I guess I owed her a debt too.

But Smith was different. Despite all the things he'd been through, he was still optimistic. I wanted him to find someone to love, just like I wanted Cami to be in a worthwhile relationship. I wished I had the power to make their lives into everything they should be, since I'd been the catalyst to most of their troubles in the first place. Now with the illness, that was something that I knew I had no control over. But every day I wished I did.

I stepped outside into the murky heat of the late-afternoon air. There was a plume of cigarette smoke to walk through on the way to the parking lot. I took a deep inhalation and drifted back to the time of my own addiction. It was reflexive, and for a moment, the lure was there. I shook it off and proceeded to my truck.

I didn't blame the smokers for standing outside doing what they needed to do to get through the day, because it was really hard to sit around and wait to hear news about your loved ones. Especially when positive news about their family and people they held dear may never come. I pushed that thought aside as well, putting one foot in front of the other until I was somewhere safe... somewhere private so I could fall apart.

I practically fell into the driver's seat, grateful for my spot near the wall in the garage, which meant no one could see me have my breakdown. I didn't have the doors on the

Jeep so it wouldn't have been hard for a person to see what was happening as my mask slipped out of place. I sat and watched as people came and went into the hospital. The longer I watched, the more I realized what kind of day each person was having. Either their faces were long and sad, beaten down from the news of the day, or they were bright and happy, like the balloons they carried with news of a new life entering the world. People were actually more predictable than they thought. Most of the time, it was fairly easy to see who a person was in the moment you met them.

For some reason, my mind moved back to the woman I'd met in the parking lot earlier that day. She was the one person who thwarted that theory—at least, I thought she did. I had to smile when I thought of her. She was so beautiful and seemed determined to have her way. And because I was society's idea of threatening, with my height, brawn, and to be frank, skin color, I had to be extra nice. That usually worked, but... Not her. No, she had me pegged. Even as she agreed to move her car, I knew she was only doing so because it was the right thing to do. Not because she showed me any deference.

From her thick coils clasped at the nape of her neck to her cool, topaz-hued skin, and even her stance, I was puzzled. The playfulness of style betrayed the seriousness in her eyes and hairstyle. And it was the most intriguing thing I'd ever seen in my life. There was something magical about it, and while I knew I had some pretty significant responsibilities with my family going on, I still wanted to know more about her. I adjusted my seat and leaned back, allowing thoughts of this woman to push away the worries of the day. I wasn't big on meditation or chakras or anything like that, but I knew I needed to let it all go for just a minute, or I was going to lose my mind.

Before I could slip too deeply into my imagination, I felt

the phone vibrate in my jacket pocket. Under normal circumstances I would let it go—there was usually nothing in those emails or text messages and phone calls or whatever the fuck that wouldn't wait until the following day, but all that had changed with my sister in the hospital. I held my breath as I pulled my cell out and looked at the screen. It wasn't a call; it was a voicemail.

I quickly navigated to voicemail and pressed the phone to my ear.

"Max, it's your boss, Jeremy. I need a real favor, man. I need you to take over 360Project for me. Dr. Greenland is out on leave unexpectedly and won't be back for quite some time. I know I promised you this summer off, but you're the only faculty member who's still in town. It would mean a lot to me, and the kids in the program."

Damn, damn, damn, I thought. Jeremy knew exactly how to get me. If it weren't for a college program much like 360Project, I wouldn't have made it so far in life.

"Shit," I murmured. While I knew the importance of it, I wasn't in the right mindset to mentor those kids, let alone the instructors. Usually, the instructors were pretty green and most of them had never been in an inner city in their lives. 360Project was kind of a jumping-off point for everyone involved, with the exception of the faculty advisor.

I spent most of my waking moments feeling guilty for shit that happened twenty-one years ago and the rest of the time just trying to get to the next day. Whether I wanted to admit it or not, I was barely holding shit together. That hadn't changed until three weeks ago when my niece and nephew had come to live with me. They were the only reason that I hadn't lost my sanity. Until I could do better, I would let my family be my guiding force, but nothing else. Not work, not women, not friends, not anything nor anyone who wasn't related to me. I needed to remember that.

But still, Jeremy had been good to me. When everything had gone down with Cami, he let me switch out my summer classes and covered the ones he couldn't find professors for himself. That wasn't the first time either. When I'd gotten my divorce, he'd let me vent for hours. By rights, he should have sent me to the employee assistance program, but he sat there, listening, offering an ear for my troubles. It was a decent thing to do, and I couldn't very well leave him in the lurch.

Opting to reply with a text message, I typed the only thing I could. "I received your voicemail. Go ahead and send me the program outline." I probably should have put something a little bit more congenial in the email, but I didn't even have energy for that.

I waited for Jeremy to respond, and when he did, I looked over the list of professors, the number of kids who'd been accepted into the six-week-long program and all the courses they were offered. Since I was to be the advisor for the program, I only had one American history course to teach. I was thankful for that. It was difficult to see the full description on my phone, so I put it away, opting to go back inside with Cami and Donnie. The fresh air had done me well because when I returned, I found I could look people in their eyes again, and even nod in greeting.

By the time I got back, the two of them were embroiled in the typical parent battle. Cami's iPad was on her lap, and Donnie had pulled the chair over to her bed and was leaning on her arm. "Wanna watch *Wednesday*?"

"How about *The Great British Bake Off*?"

"Ugh… no. They use butter and milk on that show."

"Well, I prefer you watch something that's not so dark."

"How about this?" Donnie pointed to the screen.

I walked over to the remaining chair in the room and took a seat, watching as they continued their argument.

"Oh, perfect," she said.

I heard the first chords of "ABC" by the Jackson 5 and knew they'd settled on a cartoon I'd seen the kids watching.

There was only an hour and a half left before we would have to leave and go pick up Diane from gymnastics practice. As was our routine, Cami would tell me about how her treatments were going and I would tell her about practicing in the yard with Diane and my food trials with Donnie. It was an exchange of the things that scared us both so completely but somehow helped each of us get through to the next moment. I would wait to talk about the 360Project because Cami would only worry that she was keeping me from working.

But just for a moment, I wanted her to enjoy a television show with her son by her side. It was the least I could do.

Chapter Six

TWO DATES SCHEDULED and two dates down. I hadn't liked either of those dudes. To be sure Nell couldn't call me on my eagerness to get out of our agreement, I planned to set up one more date. But that would have to wait. I had a meeting to get to on the first day of my new job.

And I was lost.

I was supposed to report to the westside ballroom, but the room numbers had no E or W to denote which side of the ballroom I was on.

I should have left earlier. But that would've meant missing the banana nut buckwheat pancakes that Nell made me for breakfast. It had been a long time since someone else made me something to eat, and I wasn't about to miss it.

I shuffled across the room, hoping to run into at least one person who would know where I was supposed to be, but no such luck so far. Since the summer semester was over, pupils and professors were scarcely found on the sprawling campus. So I had to do the best I could. Using a map I found in one of the newspaper stands around the school, I fumbled my way until I finally made it to Woodrow Wilson Hall where the ballroom was located. I glanced at my watch and found that I was already five minutes late.

It probably would've been fine if it hadn't been my first day, if I hadn't chopped all my hair off, and if the social-media-shy Prof. Wynn wasn't what appeared to be the biggest tight-ass.

Once I thankfully found where I was supposed to be, I opened the door and entered as quietly as I could, then snuck in the back to the very last table with the very last available chair. There was some perky girl sitting there who looked too young to even be in the faculty lounge but made up for it in overenthusiasm.

"Hi, I'm Candace." The blond girl stuck out her hand eagerly.

"Hi," I whispered, trying really hard not to draw attention to myself since I was apparently the last to enter the room, "I'm Quivina." I gingerly shook her hand, then laid my bag on the table and took the seat beside her.

"You'll want to grab some coffee and maybe pastry before it's too late. Prof. Wynn is about to get started. You just missed the introduction portion, so as least you don't have to worry about that." Candace waved her hand in the general direction of a table set up with all types of continental breakfast treats.

I gave her a nod, and as swiftly as I could, I made my way over to the table. No one was in my way, so I beelined to the stacked coffee cups. Maybe I wouldn't have to interact with anyone else besides this Candace person and possibly get through my day unscathed. I had a lunch date from One Cupid scheduled across campus with that guy with the genuine smile I'd seen on the app on the first night. He'd turned out to be an athletic instructor here. At least he looked to be sincere. I didn't want to get my hopes up since the first two dates had been disastrous.

I grabbed a cup and saucer and another plate with what looked like an apple Danish on it. The pickings were scarce. Thankfully, I'd eaten earlier and chose something to nibble on alongside my coffee. Setting the pastry down on the table, I placed my cup under the spicket and turned on the coffee faucet. I made every effort to move about quietly, but the cup slightly clattered against the saucer and the coffee sputtered as it poured from the urn.

"Welcome to the meeting," said a deep and husky voice that seemed like I had heard it before.

The presence was a shock and made me jump and subsequently spill my freshly poured coffee, which was remarkably hot, all over my hands. Naturally, as if to ensure I was sufficiently embarrassed, I dropped the cup and saucer.

I watched as a deep brown stain crawled over the carpet. After the commotion died down, I glanced up to find the narrowed eyes of the mean neighbor from days before.

"What the fuck?" I whisper-yelled, flinging my hands back and forth, attempting, and failing, to cool the burn on my fingers. A flush of heat ran up my neck and seared its way onto my cheeks. I wasn't sure whether I was reacting to him or the embarrassment of making such a mess.

Mean neighbor guy was saying at the same time, "I'm sorry."

"You should be. Jesus, you nearly scared me out of my skin."

Bending to gather the cup and saucer from the floor, I prayed everything hadn't been as loud as it sounded.

In another moment, he grabbed my elbow to help me upright, which was... well, not so mean. "Trust me, that was not my intent. I just wanted to introduce myself and since you were late, I didn't get a chance to."

"And who exactly are you, the hospitality police?"

"Well, it never hurts to know at least one person in a new setting."

"How do you even know I'm new here?"

"Because I've never seen you here before. Oh, and there's the other thing—you were getting luggage out of the car when I ran into you the other day."

"How could I forget that delightful encounter?" Placing the cup and saucer on the counter, I started to inspect my hand.

"Yeah... Maybe we did get off on the wrong foot." Just then, mean neighbor guy leaned forward, picking a towel up from the table. Taking my injured hand, he pressed the towel to it, then flipped it back and forth in what I assumed was an attempt to assess the damage. He dabbed the rest of the liquid away before blowing on the heated flesh. I'm sure it had the opposite effect of what he was going for, because every part of me heated up.

Releasing me, he kneeled down in front of me and wiped the tops of my boots with the napkin. Then he picked up the cup and saucer that had tumbled to the floor.

I could smell his aftershave as he stooped before me; it was like a fresh sea breeze. His locs swayed gently over his shoulder as he rolled up to face me once again. "Maybe we should use this time to start again." He took the cup and saucer and set them beside me on the tray used to discard the dirty dishes.

"Thank you. I appreciate the help," I said rather evenly, despite the flash of warmth plaguing me from the briefest contact with the stranger. He was so remarkably handsome, and I couldn't believe that I hadn't noticed exactly how much the first moment we'd met. Maybe it was because I was already so upset, but his eyes looked like molten honey, and his full lips and strong draw immediately made me think of kissing. His skin was a deep mahogany, ruddy undertones striking in the morning light shining on him through the windows. His high cheekbones took aim at his proud nose, both becoming plain in comparison to his full lips and a prominent chin dusted with the shadow of a beard. I could have gotten lost just looking at him.

His eyes roamed upward, to my hair. I'd almost forgotten that I had cut it into a curly pixie during my tequila-induced big chop. But his expression didn't change. I didn't know exactly whether that was a good or a bad thing. Some men acted as if you were half a woman if you cut off your hair.

"Anytime. Maybe after the meeting we could go grab a cup of coffee? I really am sorry... about both the other day and making you spill coffee all over yourself." He handed me a clean napkin.

"Unfortunately, I already have plans with someone. Maybe some other time."

"Maybe. I'm sure I'll see you around." He turned to walk away from me and headed for the front of the class.

I realized I hadn't even gotten his name, had no idea who he was or even why he was in the same place as me. Southeast Michigan University had offered me a position on 360Project, a program geared at prepping inner-city youths and underserved populations for the rigors of college life. I wasn't tenured anywhere, so it was my lucky break. But if this guy was going to be a coworker, maybe I would be a little more than lucky. I mean, a girl could dare to dream.

He was already talking to some other people so I didn't follow him to get his name. Instead, I returned to my seat next to Candace, who immediately started chatting my ear off about this thing or that thing. The girl was completely self-absorbed, and even though she was asking questions as if she were interested in me, they all seemed to lead back to her. It was another ten minutes of listening to her before maybe not-so-mean neighbor guy began to speak from the front of the class. But he wouldn't have been doing that... unless he...

Oh, shit.

"Hey everyone, I got a chance to meet most of you before the meeting during breakfast. But for those of you who didn't get the opportunity, my name is Professor Maxwell Wynn. I'm the dean of the historical college, and due to Professor Greenland's unexpected absence, I'll be the faculty advisor for 360Project this year. It's not a program that I am unfamiliar with, having served in it for several summers in the past. So, I don't have to tell you, it is near and dear to my heart. I too participated in a similar program for my undergrad. These kids are from neighborhoods not too far from the campus, and they look to SMU as a beacon of light amidst darkness.

"For the students that you'll encounter this summer, you have a chance to hone their desire for an education and for a better life. Such a very important job, and I fully expect each of you to be aware of that. I know how hard it is to understand and empathize with others, and for some of you, this will prove insurmountable. My expectation is that you use the six-week program to determine whether or not you have the wherewithal to deal with students who come from backgrounds very different from your own.

"There's no shame in not being able to relate. There are, however, consequences to professors who have no empathy. Usually one or two"—he said, looking around the room at each of us taking care to lock eyes with everyone—"of us won't be here for the fall semester. And that is fine. Should you find yourself among the exiting group, please feel free to reach out to me for a letter of recommendation and I'll happily give you one. Any questions on that?" Again, he looked around at each of us as if the success of the program and each adjunct in the room were the most important things in the world.

I could understand his passion for his role, but it seemed to be more than that. I had never seen anyone on the administrative side of academia have even a flicker of passion. To see someone with his tenure and obviously having been assigned the extra work of essentially babysitting the newbies, show any concern about whether we did or did not succeed? That was endearing. Perhaps it was that I had just walked onto a college campus in the role of a professor, but just a few words from him made me want to be there even more. His words made me want to help. With one glance around, I wasn't so sure everyone had interpreted his speech in the same way.

Professor Wynn, otherwise known as mean neighbor guy, cleared his throat and brought my attention back to him. "All right, then, let's go ahead with some housekeeping."

The rest of the meeting went by in a bit of a blur. We talked about all the things that we would need to facilitate the project. We went over the folders and binders and all of the materials that would be afforded us, and we discussed the computer program that would be used to provide weekly feedback to both the students and the faculty advisor, who turned out to be Prof. Wynn. He also advised us to call him Max and not Professor Wynn.

He was an efficient man, self-assured and confident in ways that made people gravitate toward him, drawn to his enigmatic charm. It was something I hadn't seen in both of our first encounters. He was the type of man who would make women want him and men envious. In the two hours that we were together, I knew that like me, most of the women in the room were thinking things that were wholly unprofessional. I tried to ignore the overwhelming desire lurking just beneath the surface. It wasn't something that I could act on, especially since technically the guy was my boss. Maybe it was just that I hadn't been attracted to someone in so long.

Either way, I was smart enough not to pee where I ate. It just wasn't prudent to date someone I worked with. Not with the need to have an income more pressing than ever before. I was depending on my own resources for the first time in my life. Besides all that, there was no inkling that he even wanted to date me. He had likely only been extending a professional courtesy when he asked me out for a cup of coffee, which was perfectly logical since I would be working with him. Most likely an olive branch and nothing more.

While I was putting all the materials that we'd been given into my brown leather messenger bag, the scent of the sea wrapping around me made me force my head up. "So, about that cup of coffee?"

He was right in front of me, all masculinity and everything that I'd been missing for so many months.

"I'm... Did you want to think about it?" His words snapped me out of my daydream and brought me back into focus with a start.

"I was just trying to think of my schedule. I mentioned I have plans already for lunch." I didn't want to be rude to Professor Wynn, but I also didn't want to stand up this guy who seemed both available, unlike my pseudo-boss, and nice, also unlike my pseudo-boss. "Maybe some other time?"

"Yeah, yeah that's fine." He waved his hand as if to indicate everything was good. "I'll catch up with you some other time. We go out as a team once every couple weeks. We'll be able to get to know each other then."

"I didn't get a chance to tell you, though. I accept your apology and agree, yes we did… We did get off to a bit of a rough start. But I have no doubt that we will have a better relationship going forward."

"No doubt." He gave me a smile. It was the type of smile that would make a woman's heart flutter. I was thankful he hadn't given me that smile before I turned him down for coffee because if he had I wouldn't have been able to refuse him.

The thought crossed my mind that Professor Max Wynn could make me act like a complete fool for him.

Chapter Seven

MAX

"WHAT'S UP BRO?" Smith said as he burst into my office without knocking, as usual.

"Nothing much. What's good with you? You're out early this morning. Aren't you usually held up in the stadium torturing your team?" Good-natured ribbing was a pastime for us.

"Nah, I've got a date." Smith looked at me, a twisted smile on his lips.

I was really happy for my younger brother. He deserved to meet someone and have the life that I was never given. I wanted the best for him. "That's good, man. Little early in the day, but to each his own. Anyone I know?"

"I don't think so. Her profile says she's new in the area, and her profile picture didn't exactly scream professor. She gave me the vibe of a fine-ass corporate lawyer. She didn't seem like the type who would hang around in your musty old library."

"You'd be surprised at all the good-looking women

hanging around in the faculty lounge. You should stop over there sometime and say it's for educational purposes." I goaded him since it was nice to see him even wanting to date someone. Not that I could talk about that to him at all. I hadn't exactly been thinking in terms of lifetime goals and long-term relationships, either. But for him... he deserved more.

My mind skipped back to Quivina Adedeji. I had procured her name from the roster and looked her up in our employee database... like a stalker. The thought made my stomach clench at the impropriety.

Smith took a seat across from me and rested his metal leg on the desk. He wasn't wearing his sports razor, the one he usually wore when he was working out with the team. I took another look and noticed the polo, khaki pants, and yellow baseball cap. It was my brother's version of fancy. "Yeah, whatever you say. I usually don't hook up with the academics. Too analytical for me. I prefer the businesswomen with their busy lives and career goals. It makes it easier when I have to go away for games."

"Oh, cool. So, all your women 'friends' fit into those neat little boxes. That's awesome." I gave him the air quotes and swallowed down the information he'd shared during a drunken night at the bar—that he didn't want to feel like a burden on anyone. That tidbit let me in on the fact that he already had an escape route planned before he got involved with anyone.

"Yeah. They are my friends. Unlike you, I enjoy having *friends*. Not being a monk who's saving myself. You should get out on a date yourself." Smith glared across the desk at me. It wasn't as if this was a new conversation for us. He was always after me to start my life over and date someone and settle down.

Of course, I was after him to do the same. But at least I'd

been married before, and it hadn't worked out the way I thought it would. I wasn't in a hurry to go down that path again. Besides, I was busy taking care of my family. Smith had just gotten over his last revision surgery when Cami had been diagnosed with her illness. And now, I didn't want him to be saddled with helping with Diane and Donnie, especially since he spent most of his life under the knife and trying to gain some semblance of normalcy. He'd had it hard enough. "I get on plenty of dates. Don't you worry about me," I said.

"The lies you tell. Diane texted me and said you walk around the house like a shadow. She's worried about you. She says nobody comes to visit, and all you do is worry about what she or her brother are up to," he said, sarcasm dripping from his every word.

"Maybe she's doing it to throw you off her trail and onto mine. Wouldn't surprise me... she's just like her mother, after all. A master at deflection."

"I think she might have a point. All you do is sit around and read historical romance novels."

"Medieval literature? Is that romance? I teach history. And how would you know anything about literature? The only books you read are on football strategies."

"Hey, man, no shade. I don't mean to be offensive. I'm just saying, you need to get out of the house every now and then. Everybody does. It's perfectly normal to have an active social life. Want to try this dating app I'm on?"

"Oh, hell no." The words came out before I could stop them.

"Why not? There's nothing wrong with narrowing the dating pool and finding singles in our area."

"You sound like an ad for the app. You can't pay for that kind of promotion."

"Ha-ha. I just think you going about this whole dating

thing too old-school. Nobody meets at church anymore. You're going to have to put yourself out there if you expect to find someone."

"See now, that's where you're wrong. I'm not looking for anybody."

"No, that's where *you're* wrong. There's a couple of different types of man in the world. There's the type who doesn't actually need anyone in their lives, because they're toxic and patriarchal. And then there's your type. You deserve someone special. You are a man who deserves everything. But one day, you won't have us to look after anymore. What will you do then?"

Smith wasn't exactly the type of person to be sentimental. He'd never said anything remotely that warm to me before. And here we were. I didn't know what to say. I knew he was trying to be kind, but I also knew it wasn't true. I didn't deserve shit. I hadn't done anything to help my family before. In fact, I had caused their downfall. I don't know why Smith couldn't see that. "Once Cami's okay, I'll think about it." Yeah, I was lying, but he didn't need to know that.

"Why do I feel like you're just saying that to get me off your back?"

"Come on, man. Shouldn't you be heading out for your date?"

"Okay, whatever. You're right, but I wanted to make sure our niece and nephew didn't kidnap you and put you in a dumpster. Where are they, anyway?"

"Diane's in gymnastics and Donnie's in science camp. They will be there until the middle of the afternoon. If you wanna see them, we'll be home around four or five."

"I'll make more of an effort to do that. I haven't seen them this week at all. They need all of us in their lives. I'll try to take them to get some ice cream. And if you need me to, just let me know if they want to spend the night with me. That way, Uncle Max can go get a life."

The jab didn't escape my attention.

"Oh, that's what we're doing," I said, tossing him a wink. "I'm going to go get some lunch. I didn't get a chance to eat this morning because I was talking to the new faculty members. I'm heading over to Hop Cat. You need a ride?"

"Yeah, that would be cool. That's where my date is. Thanks, bro."

Smith didn't drive, not because he couldn't, but because he was that much of an athlete. He usually rode a bike or jogged wherever he went. He put me to shame with his dedication to physical health. Before the accident, he was going to be an NFL player. He had been so good that it didn't matter if most student athletes never made it that far. He would have, and I was the reason that he had not. "All right, give me a second. I just gotta shoot this email off."

"Cool, I'll head downstairs and meet you by your car."

I sent the reminder about the syllabus to all of the professors on the summer program, then put everything away, all the folders and the materials that I had given out to the faculty members. I was supposed to start working on the textbook orders, but since half of them hadn't come in yet from adjunct team members, it could wait. I had to eat, after all. And Donnie's vegan diet plan left me feeling hungry most of the time. I grabbed my keys and my hat, and hurried down the stairs after Smith, happy that for once, maybe, he would get exactly what he deserved.

It didn't take a long time for us to make it over to Hop Cat, a restaurant brewery in Midtown Detroit not too far from the university. As a place where most of my students went during the school year, it had become a favored spot for most people in the area. I parked the car, and Smith and I headed inside.

"You see who you're waiting on?" I asked.

"I don't know. The avatars and profile pictures are usually pretty small. But she says she'll be wearing a white dress with roses, a denim vest, and red sandals."

That was funny. That was the exact same way I would have described Quivina from earlier at our meeting. I never noticed things like that, but I had wiped her shoes off for her and couldn't help but notice what she wore on the way down, among other things. The only difference was she had on black booties or whatever Diane had called them. Most likely wasn't the same girl. Hell, most of the time women shopped according to the trend and they all looked the same. Still, I was a bit concerned that it was the same person. "You want me to help you look for her?"

"Nah, I can find a woman fine on my own. You go ahead and get your lunch. I know you got a busy day ahead of you." Smith wasn't even paying attention to me anymore. He was busy looking around the room to see if he spotted his mystery girl.

I knew the feeling. I probably would've been doing the same thing. "Cool. I may have something going, so I'll text you to let you know what's up."

We dapped one another up, then I turned to the bar to place my to-go order. The bartender, Melinda, was the same girl I always saw working there when I stopped by, and she gave me an easy smile when I walked up.

"Hey, Max." Melinda was a tall, fair-skinned beauty. Her long hair was pulled back into a sleek ponytail and she wore the black-and-white jersey-style shirt for the uniform. She always looked wonderful, a warm smile on her face every time I saw her. She wasn't my type, but she was nice, nonetheless.

"Hey, Melinda. I'll take my usual," I said.

"Coming right up." She turned to punch the cheeseburger medium well and fries into the system.

As she did, I turned around and looked back in the direction of my brother. Smith was smiling and had started slowly walking toward the dining room area. I couldn't see who he was looking at because the bar was tall and covered most of the dining area. But he was saying hello. I could read his lips from where I sat.

I leaned back to see if I could catch a glimpse of who he was meeting. I hoped she was pretty, and funny. More than anything, though, I hoped that she understood having an amputation didn't mean a person didn't deserve love.

In another instant, I saw the blue denim against the white dress emerge from behind the bar. Smith extended his hand and took hers, enclosing it between both of his. As soon as I saw the heart-shaped mass of coils dancing around her head, the wide smile, her beautiful body, I knew. I guess I had known as soon as he described her.

It was Quivina.

And even though I wanted my brother to have every happiness, I felt whatever had been brewing in my chest crack in half.

Chapter Eight

WHAT. The. Fuck.

I'd just seen my blind date, well almost blind date—I guess I could call him the app date—walking with my new boss. Mean neighbor guy seemed to be very, very chummy with app date guy. In what universe does that happen? And why would it happen to me? My hand moved instinctively to my mouth, despite having kicked the nail-biting habit in college. Instead of returning to old habits, though, I folded my hands on my lap and waited for him to see me.

I had half a mind to get up and run out of the place. I didn't need that kind of drama in my life. Mean neighbor guy had asked me on a date to go have coffee with him. Although... Was he really asking me on a date, or was I making more out of it than it actually was? It was quite possible that I was overreacting. He was the type of man who could easily cause overreactions in a woman.

I decided to go ahead, take the bull by the horns, and get up and go over to introduce myself to the person I was actually there to meet. He was a good-looking guy, and granted I didn't get the same type of physical reaction to him that I did with Max, but he was cute. On the app, his screen name was Mr. Smith. I did love the anonymity of One Cupid because it kept us from those awkward instances where we knew each other's name and personal details and ended up not liking the person at all. I didn't want to have to go through the process of extricating myself from a relationship that had gone south when we weren't even at first base.

Mr. Smith wore khakis, a polo, and gym shoes, so I knew he was a casual type of guy. He had already told me that he was a below-the-knee amputee. I could see the metal exposed between the hem of his khakis and the top of his gym shoe. He didn't see him at all bothered by having an amputation and had been very open about it during our text conversation through the application.

He told me he'd been in a car accident, shared that there were still times when revisions were needed to make corrections to his stump, and told me that it was a battle he was never really going to be done with. It was just a fact of life for him. He had been so open and honest with me about his amputation that he had made it easy for me to share my big-chop hair journey.

Not that the two were synonymous in any way. My decision to cut off my hair and start again as my natural self was a choice. Mr. Smith, on the other hand, had no choice in the matter. From what I understood, his accident had been caused by someone else's negligence. While he hadn't told me who, I could understand how it would feel to have all of your choices taken away from you. I had gone through similar things with nearly everything in my life—my father, my ex, my culture—yet I'd never had such an optimistic outlook. His optimism reminded me that none of my past hurts needed to define me.

No matter who Mr. Smith had been standing with, I very much wanted to meet him. I was even happier that I'd changed into my sassy sandals. I wanted him to see the image I'd portrayed online. Not the late-on-her-first-day, disowned-by-her-father, cheated-on, and divorced me. I wanted him to meet girl-on-a-mission and a-new-purpose-in-life me. So, I'd gone home and replaced my work-appropriate footwear, donned some red lipstick, and sprayed more leave-in conditioner on my curls to refresh them, all the while praying I looked confident even if I didn't feel it.

I stood, smoothing my dress, and took the first step toward him. Thankfully, Max headed off in the direction of the bar and my date's eyes found mine while I was on my way. Giving him a wave, I put on my best smile. The option to flee the scene now gone, I closed the distance between us. "Mr. Smith, it's me."

"MA101?"

"Yup that's me. I'm glad I got the right person. Your screen name almost sounds like it's made up." I laughed awkwardly, trying my best not to sound like a weirdo.

"Well, it is actually made up." He chuckled. Mr. Smith had that suave factor, like every good jock, hero, motorcycle-riding badass. I knew he had been "cool" in his day, even though from the looks of him, I have a couple years on him. We hadn't discussed age, but I was sure Mr. Smith was about a decade younger than me. Shouldn't have been a problem, because we weren't talking wedding bells. We were just meeting up to have a good time. Maybe if it led to something else, we would worry about the hard parts—the age thing, the logistics of dating, and all the other stuff that comes along with starting relationships. For now, though, we would take it easy.

"I have a seat over here in the back. Some booth out of the way and away from the noise of the bar. I hope that's okay?" I waved to the area I'd secured for our date and nodded my head in that direction.

"Yeah, yeah that's absolutely fine." He extended a hand and allowed me to lead the way.

I gave him another smile because I couldn't help it—he was the type of person who made you feel good. Once we made it to the table, I took my seat on the side against the wall and he sat opposite me.

"So, my real name is Smith Wynn," he said, once he got comfortable.

I, on the other hand, nearly bit my tongue off. Wynn. As in Maxwell Wynn.

"You mean... You mean, Maxwell is your brother?" I asked the question with trepidation. How sticky would that be? I wouldn't say my relationship with Max was anything beyond colleague. We'd had too much of a rocky start for anything other than professional courtesies, regardless of his presentation style being... well, not what I'd expected.

His brows screwed down as he considered my question for a moment. "Yeah. He's my brother, and we have different moms, but we never... We never think about the differences."

"Oh," I said, trying really hard to keep the alarm out of my tone.

"God. You didn't used to date him, did you?"

"No," I replied, a bit too enthusiastically. It was the truth, but that didn't mean I hadn't had vividly sexual, sporadic, and nasty thoughts about him. "We work together."

"You work at SMU too?"

"I do. I just started as an adjunct professor there this week."

"So you'll be in the 360Project?"

"Yeah, I'm really excited about it. But that's how I know Max. He's the faculty advisor for this term."

"He mentioned that to me. He must not have seen you, though. Because he absolutely would have tried to date you."

A heated rush covered me, leaving my face on fire at his words. I took a sip of my water and gave a slight smile. So many things stacked up against anything coming out of that relationship. First, he was technically my boss for at least a semester, then he was mean at times. I didn't need another surly man in my life, that was for sure. And why was I even pondering any of those things? I was having lunch with a man who seemed perfectly nice and charming. Win-win, right? "I can tell who got all the charm in the family."

"Max tries to keep up with me. But some people are just born with it. I remind him I'm the one blessed with the appeal all the time." The corners of his eyes crinkled with his smile. Smith seemed to be a person who didn't have to work for his happiness. Even knowing him for only a few minutes, I already envied that of him.

"And you're modest too. Look at that." I tossed him a wink.

"I tried reticence once. It didn't fit."

"I'll have to remember that about you."

"So, you look like the type of woman with a story. What made you move back from *Hot-lanta* to Detroit? There's got to be something behind that. And don't tell me it was for the lovely weather." Smith looked at me as if he was truly ready to listen and would hang onto my every word. It was as if he was gently encouraging me to share my troubles. And I wanted to because I'd never told anyone my whole story. Not even Nell.

"Well to be perfectly honest, my ex-husband was a bastard. I wish there was a better way to say that. Or something that would justify me being with him in the first place. But my culture—"

"Okay, I wanted to ask ever since I heard you speak, but that's so rude. But where are you from?"

"We moved to Michigan from Nigeria when I was six years old. I'm almost embarrassed to say, but I haven't been back there since I was a teenager. Although I will go back to visit eventually."

"I'm sorry. I shouldn't have cut you off. It's just that I could listen to you speak all day... and all night."

Smith was very complimentary, and I wished I felt something akin to desire... but I didn't.

"Usually, my name is a giveaway," I said. Smith gave me a questioning look, indicating he didn't know, either. "I guess you don't have my real name." The anonymity of internet dating was easy to forget. "I'm Quivina Adedeji. Anyway, being from Nigeria, your parents have a lot to do with your choices of a spouse, especially old-school parents like mine. They knew Kenyon, and they knew his family. When he became a surgeon, it was pretty much a done deal. So, when we graduated, I married him and we traveled wherever his residency sent him. Now, he lives in Atlanta with his new girlfriend, and I live here."

Smith gave me a look as if he completely understood what I was saying to him. Although, he couldn't possibly. Most African Americans didn't have to deal with old-school, patriarchal norms. Not that they should have to deal with that on top of the rest of their, rather our, struggles. I was no stranger to racism, nor sexism, and certainly not discriminatory practices. Like we all were. But being disowned by family members for getting a divorce didn't seem to be a shared concern. At least...

"Well, his loss is my gain, huh?" He chuckled, and I knew the statement was not meant to be flippant. It was obvious he wanted to lighten the mood and perhaps in some way to let me know that he did actually understand what I was referring to.

"I guess. But my father doesn't see it that way. He can only see me as the idiot who let a surgeon go."

"Still, seems a shame to have to deal with your parent's expectations on top of your divorce."

"Yeah. He doesn't seem to notice that I'm a doctor. I don't need to land one. Although not a medical doctor, it takes a lot to get a PhD in physics." My eyeroll was completely involuntary.

"That's quite an accomplishment. In physics, no less. I always sucked at math."

"And I always sucked at everything else." The shared chuckles led us to talk more, slowly dissolving into easy conversation. It was almost a surprise when the waitress walked up to us.

We put in our orders, and I tried to hide my amazement at exactly how much food he ordered. My ruse utterly failed since he explained the whole macronutrient regimen to me the moment our waitress left us.

In fact, we were carrying on like people who'd known one another for much longer than just under thirty minutes. Smith provided recommendations for mocktail pairings for my meal, since I told him I wasn't a big day-drinker. Truth be told, I was such a lightweight, the last thing I needed was to be tipsy on my first day of work.

"You two seem to be having a good time." While the question came from behind me, I knew exactly who it was.

"You should join us, man." Smith was looking over my shoulder as he spoke.

Though I wanted to keep staring at Smith so I didn't have to face Maxwell, I accepted my fate and turned around.

He didn't look at all thrilled to find me seated across from his brother.

"Hi again, Professor Wynn." My voice came out breathier than I had intended.

"Hi, Quivina. Remember, it's Max. And no thanks, guys, I gotta get back to start loading the schedules into the system." He shifted on one foot and shoved one of his hands in his pockets before coming to stand between the two of us at the table.

"All work and no play. Don't you have an admin for that?" Smith gave his brother an incredulous look.

"I do. But I prefer doing it myself. I'm kind of hands-on like that."

As he said the words, a shiver ran through me, the involuntary tremble of my shoulders. Fortunately, I don't think either of them saw.

"Whatever you say. I just don't want to see you go to burnout. At least you got something to eat, which is already an improvement," Smith said.

"I have to eat with our niece and nephew. I can't chase them around and play chauffeur without having some fuel. And on that note, I'll let you two get back to your date." Max walked away without looking back at the table.

"Have a good day," I said.

He never broke his stride.

"Don't worry about him. He's like that with everyone."

My confusion must've shown on my face, because it was as if Smith was consoling me. "No, it's fine. I'm sure he's in a rush." I shouldn't have been so obvious with my dejection after Max left.

"Hey, I was thinking... You want to go somewhere with me? I mean, later on tonight ?"

"Two dates on the same day? I don't think I've ever done that before. Like a two-for-one special."

Smith snickered at my little joke. "Think of it as a continuation." Smith looked at me, and his wide smile went to something a little bit sultrier. And he was an attractive man, who someone could spend all their time watching.

"Yes," I said.

"Good. Because I have something special I want you to see," he said. "We can Lyft over."

"Oh, I have a car. I could drive us."

"Now that's very Gen X."

"Well, considering I am Gen X, that makes sense." Shit, we never even talked about ages. I knew he was younger than me from the onset, and he had to know I was a little older than him... right?

"Get out. You don't even look thirty-five."

"Charming ass," I said, trying not to blush again.

"Some say, but if you ask the players about Coach Wynn, they'll tell you a different story."

I could see myself beginning to like Smith. But my mind wouldn't let me forget about Max, not even for a moment. He disarmed me, whatever passed between us both unnerving and intriguing. He was exactly the type of man I didn't need at the moment.

Chapter Nine

I DON'T EVEN KNOW how long Smith and I were out.

We went everywhere, and everywhere we went we had fun. It was a night of food, merriment, and dancing. Everything would have been perfect, but he felt more like a good friend.

Of course, that's what you want in a mate. But a bit of passion would've been nice too.

I pulled up to the front walkway of his apartment building, a bit more rustic than the contemporary building that Max and Nell lived in. Somehow, though, it seemed very much like something Smith would choose. He was an athlete and an all-around laid-back person, so the large brick building suited him.

"This is me." He pointed at the building as I slowed down upon approach.

"It's cute," I said.

"Yeah, it's home."

"Well, I had a good time tonight. Probably more fun than I should have. It's going to take me forever to turn in that syllabus for work." I ran my hand through my hair, still shocked by the shorter length. It was the force of habit, really. Nothing was hanging in my eyes or tickling my neck, so I wasn't sure why I did it. The moment I realized what I'd done, I grew self-conscious. I mentally attempted to knock the negative record playing over and over in my mind off track.

"I'm glad you had a good time. But you seem... almost a little sad now. I hope it's just because the date is ending." Smith's voice was low and comforting with a bit of hope tinged at the end.

"No, no. I was just thinking about all the things I have to do, that's all. And yeah, a bit of me does hate that the date is ending, though. That's what we get for going out on a weeknight like kids."

"Don't knock being a kid. That was the best time of my life."

I wondered for a moment whether part of his response was because he hadn't been an amputee until he was fifteen. I could imagine most men would find it hard to lose part of themselves, especially one so critical to how your life was supposed to turn out. He was supposed to be a football player and he'd shared with me earlier in the evening how hard it was for him to come to terms with the fact that he probably never would be. And he confessed that he had a little envy for the younger players who were still able to follow their dreams despite having amputations. "Yeah, well, I was a skinny nerd girl from another country who all the kids teased. I didn't really enjoy my teenage years as much as you did, someone who was so popular and probably had an insane effect on the young women you went to school with."

"I did, I did. But I've always been the one-girl-at-a-time type. It's too much trouble to cheat and I just find it better, personally. If I had a creed, that would be it."

"Hmmm. You know I've never thought of giving myself a creed. You do mean like a motto, right?"

"Yeah, like your words to live by. What would yours be?"

I pondered for a moment, trying to figure it out, and honestly, I drew a blank. That was quite a question for someone who had never done anything for themselves, at all. It would have been nice to know exactly who I was and what I wanted at a younger age. Forty-five was a little late to be starting over, but here I was. "I think I'm going to have to get back to you on that, Smith. Can you give me a couple of days?"

"Take all the time you need, lady. You don't want to rush your creed. That's something that needs your full attention. I know a guy once who had the wrong creed... he ended up with a tattoo of an iguana on his face. True story." His hearty laugh blended in with mine.

I was leaning over the center console of my car and found myself face-to-face with Smith. The mood couldn't have been more romantic if it were a Hollywood movie.

He must have felt the same way because he leaned in closer too. Our eyes locked, and the tinkling laughter fell away. I should have wanted to kiss him, but... damned if his brother's face didn't pop into my mind. I already knew the reasons Maxwell and I couldn't be together, so this kiss should have been the salve I needed to remind myself I was still desirable, that someone still wanted me. Resolute in my decision, I leaned in, puckered my lips, and closed my eyes.

Salve it was not, however. Somehow, we managed to bump foreheads.

"Ouch." I rubbed at the pain in my forehead from our collision.

"I'm so sorry. I can assure you that nothing like this has ever happened to me." Smith looked genuinely apologetic, even if he also swiped a hand over his head.

"I'm gonna go ahead and take that as a hint. I'll kiss you in a much better way anyway." He lifted my hand in his, bringing my knuckles to his soft, warm lips. He pressed his mouth to my hand, and I swear my heart pulled. "That still works, right?"

"Oh yeah. It works just fine," I said, impressed by his chivalry.

"I hope to see you real soon, Q."

We had agreed upon nicknames somewhere around the skate park. He was an avid skateboarder and had taken me to his favorite place near campus. "I hope to see you soon too, Pronto." Pronto was Smith's nickname from his high school football days. He said some of the SMU team still called him that. Coach Pronto, at least. He was somewhat of a legend, even though he'd only played in high school for a couple of years.

"So, when do you want to go out again, since the feeling is mutual?"

"Text me before the weekend, and maybe we can do something then."

"I'll do that. Have a good night." He climbed out of my Audi and gently closed the door as if it were something precious. I watched as he made his way to the front door. I'd spent an entire evening with this man observing his life with him taking me around and showing me everything that mattered to him. I'd even seen the old house near Palmer Park from when he was a child. It was beautiful, a grand home with enough backyard for three rambunctious children. It wasn't much different from my own home, as I'd grown up in a similar neighborhood not too far away. He should have been perfect for me, but... something just wasn't there.

On the drive home, I thought over everything that had happened on our date. We had so much fun, wasting time and getting to know one another. Is that what dating was supposed to be? It had been a great date, if I were to be honest with myself. And if I would have felt anything remotely passionate it would have been even better. Then again, what would I know of passion? I had only been with my ex-husband and a few dates before that. Kenyan was my first. A man chosen by my father and one who had not spent a great deal of time exploring what I wanted or needed.

I wondered how soon was appropriate before considering sleeping with a man. Or did I even want to sleep with Smith? How could I be a self-proclaimed feminist when I had no idea what I wanted for myself?

I pulled into the parking lot and took the extra spot Nell had secured for me so I wouldn't cause any more parking wars. Residents used the area for visitors, and while it was a good distance away from the front door, it was better than parking several streets over, given the limited space. I parked the car and made my way up, all the while pondering all the events of the day. I wanted to have my thoughts organized before I shared them with Nell. She was going to want details and was probably sitting up there right now with her glass of Jesus juice, as she called it, waiting for me to tell all.

I used my key to let myself in, and it was only a matter of minutes before I was standing in the entryway waiting to be accosted with questions.

Nell didn't disappoint. She rounded the corner in overly fluffy house shoes, housecoat and comfy nightgown draped around her thin frame. She had two empty glasses in her hands and extended one out to me, then motioned to the couch. "Come on, girl. I know you got that juice. And I'm ready to hear it."

"Eager for the tea, are we?" I followed her across the room, and we landed on the couch. She filled her glass, set it down on the table, and began to pour mine.

"Tea is what you dish out when it's gossip about others. You can't gossip about yourself, right? So, this is juice." The statement accompanied by her completely confident expression made it difficult to argue her point.

"Oh, I see. I need to keep up with my street vernacular." I rolled my eyes and accepted the fresh pour.

"I will spend all the time in the world talking about the difference between tea and juice, as long as you give me all the details about that good-looking man you spent so much time with. It's almost tomorrow. I almost called the cavalry in."

No one could accuse Nell of being understated. "Okay, fine. I'll tell you. He was the perfect gentleman. I laughed so much my cheeks hurt. He took me everywhere—like, did you know there's a spot at the top of the Fort Street Bridge on I75 where you can see the entire skyline of Detroit? It was so beautiful. We drove over that bridge two times. Even though it smells so bad near the plants. He is such a cool dude."

"Oh, that sounds really fine... But... You don't seem like it was a love connection." Nell stared at me with her head tilted to the side. Her expression held her skepticism, like she knew what I was thinking. As well she should since she had known me since I was a little girl.

"Well, our kiss was so wrong. When I say it went left, I mean it literally. Instead of our lips connecting, we bumped heads." Instinctively, I ran my hand over my forehead.

"Oh, girl. That is not good. But a lot of things that start

off bad… you just have to try it again. Do you…you know, want to try again? Think it'll be worth it?"

"I don't know. There's one other thing I need to tell."

"I knew you were holding back on something. Spill it."

"He is mean neighbor dude's brother…" I paused, taking a page from Nell's dramatic effect book. "And if I'm being honest, I felt more chemistry from him than from Smith."

"This is bad. I mean this is not good, right?"

"I don't know. Mean neighbor guy—his name is Max, by the way—and I don't seem to get along well. I always feel awkward around him. He's my boss for 360Project, kind of… I report to the Dean of Mathematics and Sciences starting in the fall, but I guess he's on some sabbatical this summer. And aside from inviting me to coffee, he's almost icy. Like, I get that whole hot-then-cold thing with him. And that's not, despite how I've been acting, attractive at all for me. I don't want a relationship that reminds me of teen movies from the '80s."

"No, and he's your boss for the summer… that's a serious no-go, right?"

"Yeah, that too. Smith seems way more relaxed. And as far as Max is concerned, I'm probably making a big deal out of nothing. He probably asks everyone to go for coffee with him… You know, as the faculty advisor."

"My stodgy, old-ass advisors have never asked me on a coffee break. So, there's probably something to it. But if you two aren't getting along already, why rock the boat? I know how hard it is for you to find a job in academia when you don't have much experience. There's no sense in risking that just to get you a piece."

"Ugh! Since when did you start talking like a dirty old sailor?"

"Well, you know… I dated that naval officer about a year

and a half ago. But she had nothing to do with my dirty mouth. You know full well I've been plenty filthy since the day you met me." She tipped her head back and howled, her feet raising from the floor and folding them beneath her as she leaned in to reengage. "But for real, though, you don't have to make these choices right now. It's perfectly fine for you to just date Smith while you figure out what, if anything, you want to do with Max. That's your prerogative."

"Pretty sure you're just quoting songs now."

"Ain't nothing wrong with that. Bobby Brown was spitting fire."

"What would your tenure committee say if they heard you out here lifting passages for lectures?"

"They'd say 'she ready.'" She snapped her fingers as she raised her hands in the air.

"Oh, Lord. Anyway, I honestly don't have a problem yet. Max is a coworker. And if I can't get past first base with Smith, it would be a non-issue even if he wasn't."

"That may be. But it could get sticky."

"Let's just hope it doesn't come to that. Max and Smith already have a tenuous relationship and I don't want to make it worse." I certainly hoped I wouldn't.

Chapter Ten

MAX

I THINK I got even angrier when I realized Quivina hadn't sent in her syllabus. Smith texted me when he finally made it home late that night to tell me it was a *good* date. I knew what good meant for Pronto. Had he actually been on a second date with her on the same day? Seemed excessive for two people who'd just met. *Or you're just jealous...*

The thing I needed to get clear on was whether I was mad because I didn't want her dating my brother or because we had less than a week to get ready for 360Project. She wasn't my woman... she was barely a friend. She was actually just my coworker. I would be her faculty advisor for the duration of the term. I knew I had no business whatsoever trying to lay claim to her, even mentally.

What made matters worse was I had been the person responsible for Smith's life ending up the way it had. I should've been cheering for him... if they were hitting it off. I wanted my brother to be happy, and I for damn sure didn't want any more strife between us. It had been years and years since we'd even had an argument. It had taken us what seemed like forever to rebuild our relationship. While I still had regrets, they had always been about me. Never once had they been about some external factor, and that was something I could feel happening now, even if I hadn't actually done anything.

I still remembered the day. The rain... the argument with my father over picking Smith up from practice. I'd acted like a petulant brat... not like the grown-ass man I should have been. We'd still been arguing when I picked him up. I was talking to my father on my cell, back in the days before *no texting and driving* campaigns and software in cars to make calls hands-free. One snap at my father, one glance away from the road to snap at Smith who was asking us not to argue, and everyone's life changed. Those moments ended Smith's football career and my father's life.

But now this woman, this woman I barely knew, was making me rage. The morning had started crappy. I'd spilled my coffee beans all over the floor, my email was starting in safe mode, then something in the office smelled like cheese, and not in a good way.

I had been waiting for my email to open on my desktop for over thirty minutes. I could access my work email from my phone, but I didn't want to make the mistake of sending Quivina errors or typos indicative of mobile communications. There's nothing worse than being snarky and finding typos in your correspondence.

I sat there glaring at my computer screen waiting for IT to come over and fix it. It took them another thirty minutes to get there and less than five seconds to fix what was ailing my system.

"Thanks, Duncan," I said to our resident IT guy. Duncan was about my height but half my size. He always struck me as a bit odd. Perhaps eccentric was the better word since he wore horn-rimmed glasses and button-down shirts with ties every single day. It was like working with someone out of the seventies.

"No problem, Professor Wynn. You just have to log out of your system every night to make sure that any available upgrades make it onto your hard drive and that will help your system function properly. Last night we had to run a virus scan on the entire network. There was a malware virus that attacked the science department. I spent more of the night pushing through the updated security protocol. Because your system was just locked, it didn't reach you in time. Anyone whose system wasn't updated was forced into safe mode." Duncan said the words matter-of-factly.

And even though he was completely competent and absolutely correct in my need to log off every single night, I found myself wanting to get away. "I'll try to remember that, Duncan," I said. It wasn't his fault that Quivina was going out with my brother either.

Once my computer was up, I struggled with what kind of email to actually send her. I didn't know whether to start off with niceties or to keep the conversation strictly business. My gut told me to be stern, but I couldn't very well treat Quivina like anything other than a respected team member. Fuck, I needed to get my head on straight.

In the end, and after starting six or seven emails, I had to consider whether or not I would do that with anyone else. The resolution was of course no, because I wasn't jealous over anyone else.

Dear Quivina,

I was looking forward to reviewing your syllabus; however, I haven't received it yet. I would like to ensure that the books for the students are available by Monday morning. Since most of the students can't afford textbooks out of pocket, it becomes imperative that we place the order and have them available by the time they reach classrooms next week. The students deserve the best we have to offer. Let's ensure the best is what they receive.

I appreciate your attention to this matter, in advance.
Best,
M. Wynn

I hit send and immediately regretted it. Dammit, should I have added best? It sounded like a code word for "screw you," like "regards." I'd been asking myself that question for the last hour and a half, and the only thing that made it better was that my slow-brew coffee was finally finished. I was able to focus and get a little bit of work done, despite refreshing my inbox constantly.

By the time I heard the knock on the door, I'd put in the order for the rest of the textbooks and emailed the confirmations over to Valerie, my administrative assistant.

"Who is it?" It was still a bit too early for it to be any of the faculty. I requested that they be in by ten on days when they didn't have classes. It was probably Valerie. I had most likely made a mistake on the order due to my distraction.

"It's Quivina Adedeji."

Her voice raised the hair on my arms, and my heart banged inside my ribs, followed by a knot pulsing in my stomach. It was like sitting up too fast after a night of tequila. Goddamn, I needed to pull myself together.

"Come in, please," I said, trying my hardest not to sound like a psychopath. There was nothing normal about having that type of reaction to someone I barely knew. I had to check myself because I could feel a little boy inside pitching a fit because his marbles had been messed with. Fuck, they weren't my marbles in the first place.

She stepped into the room, and it immediately filled with the scents of lilacs and honey. "Hi there, Max. Good morning. I wanted to stop by in person and tell you how sorry I am. I sent the syllabus over last night, but when I got here I found that my email had not gone out. It was sitting as a draft in my outbox. For some reason, my Outlook is in safe mode."

Fuck me. Well, thank goodness I hadn't gone completely off in the email. But that didn't stop me from feeling like a world-class asshole for immediately assuming she'd been so enamored with my brother, she hadn't done her job. I had to wonder whether I would have rushed to judge anyone else so quickly No matter what, I was always, always fair. "Oh yeah, I'm so sorry. I just found out this morning that there was some kind of virus over in the science department. I guess I uh... didn't put that together," I stammered. Yup, I was a dick. "Your computer was impacted the same way mine was. Let me guess, you just locked it?" In an effort to lighten the tension in the room, I attempted a smile. As I waited for her response, I couldn't help but stare at her lovely face, and even though the sun wasn't shining directly on her, her eyes seemed to illuminate her soul. Despite my efforts the strain between us persisted. I knew I shouldn't have put *best* in that email.

"Am I in trouble for that too? Apparently, in addition to not sending over my syllabus as required, I failed in the way I shut off my computer." Quivina's eyes narrowed as she glared at me. I hoped she wasn't actually pissed.

"We run a tight ship around here." I nearly coughed on the last of the sentence because my chest felt constricted. I wasn't sure how, since I was technically her superior, but I could feel myself squirm under her disapproval. Everything inside me wanted to turn the situation around—to somehow please her, though I shouldn't have. Not only was she dating my brother, but I was essentially her boss. Both of those factors practically etched *off-limits* into her skin like a tattoo.

"I'll have to remember that. But since my computer is still down, I can write down the name of the book for you so you don't have to wait for me to get my email. The ISBN is on here." She waved a yellow sticky note in my direction. She stepped over, and I noticed the flouncy bottom of her skirt. She always dressed as if she were going to a lovely day party or one of those women's brunches.

I reached up and accepted the note from her. Ever since she'd cut her hair, I had truly been able to see her. It was as if God himself had fashioned her the perfect face. Full lips and eyes wide and sultry made me want to run a finger down the curves of her face just to see if she was real.

"Thank you for bringing this by." I cleared my throat and attempted to jolt myself back into reality. This was about to be my brother's girl. I shouldn't imagine anything about her, not the way she would look in the morning after we just made love or how she would look with my body pressed against hers as I stared down into her eyes. "I'll get this in the system. You can call the IT guy, Duncan, and he'll come by and get your system going."

"Thank you, Professor Wynn. I'll call him now." Quivina turned around and walked toward the door. While I wasn't exactly sure why, my chest tightened as she glanced back over her shoulder at me.

"It's Max, remember?"

"I do. It's just habit. My bad. Anyway, I'll see you later." She gave a wave before disappearing behind my office door.

The moment she was gone, the room felt empty and

gray. It was like all the vibrancy in the air wasn't able to stick around after she showed it what it was missing.

I got up and went over to grab some more coffee. I was drinking too much of it these days but I'd been burning it on both ends, trying to accommodate the kids and make sure they saw their mom regularly. They seemed to appreciate it... most of the time. As a result, there was barely any coffee left. It would take hours to brew a fresh batch. And I did not have hours, because I had to walk over to meet the dean to reassure him that everything was going to go off without a hitch.

The soft knock at the door was like déjà vu. This time though, there was no waiting for me to answer.

Quivina stuck her head in the room, the knock coming simultaneously. "Hello again." She gave me a wide smile. "I saw you had some coffee in here. This stuff in the kitchen is so gross. If it's not too much of a bother, I was hoping I could grab some of yours?"

"Oh, yeah, sure." As soon as I said it, I wondered how soon I could get in to see a therapist. I had never willingly given up the last bits of my coffee stash.

"Thanks so much." She walked back into the room, bringing back all the color and vivacity that had previously been there. "One of my friends in college used to make it this way. Of course, he was Colombian, and his parents were coffee farmers so we just chalked it up to him being a perfectionist. I never thought I'd see another single person doing it this way again. And then I met you." She kind of guffawed at that, lifting her giant mug and setting it on the table. Printed on the front in white lettering were the words *Coffee is the C in my MC squared.*

I couldn't help but notice I didn't have to tell her how to keep the beans from falling out into her cup with the coffee. She was a pro already.

"So, I'm probably the second greatest coffee lover you've ever met."

"Oh no. You're the third. I am hardcore," she said, raising her brows a touch. The light, airy sound of her giggles tinkled around the room, and she exposed her neck to me. Her soft, curly hair danced as she rocked a bit back and forth. She continued to giggle as she poured cream into her coffee, then she turned around to face me, leaning her voluptuous ass against the countertop. I'd never been so jealous of an inanimate object in my life. "So, Max, I forgot to ask you if we were able to take the kids places."

"We can, we just have to be really careful since some of the kids could be under the age of eighteen. For that reason, we generally have offsite study sessions until the 300 series courses when they are a bit older and a little more ready to handle being outside of the classroom."

"I see. I was just wondering."

"Well, what did you want to do?" I asked, curiosity getting the better of me.

"I wanted to take them to see a movie. *The Theory of Everything*—it's Stephen Hawking's story. When I was a kid, I wasn't allowed to watch a lot of movies. I kind of stumbled into math. It would've been nice if someone would've guided me in that direction. That's what I'm hoping to do for these kids this summer."

"I get that. Most kids learn how to feel about something based on their adult role model's reactions to it, right?"

"Exactly. And most people treat math like the plague."

I had to laugh because I knew she was right. "Yeah, well, try being a history professor."

"Yeah. I see what you mean."

The tension in the air lifted around us. Our conversation was flowing easy and free. It was the first time, for us anyway. I almost wanted to knock on wood to make sure it stayed that way. "Yup. For that reason, we must try to ensure that all of history is included in their education. Not just the commonly known history bites but also history that isn't widely shared in the educational sphere."

"You don't have to go any further on that. I completely understand. I was nearly eighteen by the time I found out about all the contributions African Americans had made to the US. Since I wasn't from here, I wouldn't have even known where to start."

"I had a really good history teacher. While the curriculum could be restrictive, he had a way of slipping it in that kept us engaged and made us want to know more."

"Well, that's awesome," Quivina said.

"Yes, he was. But I think your idea is great... maybe we could do a creative project around those people who inspired us and sparked a love of our subject area. You think maybe a weekly theater night would help bring the students together and ensure that they saw a representation of what motivated us?"

"I hadn't really thought about it being a project, but that is even better. What can we do? This sounds so fun." Her face lit up in that special way, just like when she smiled at me.

"I don't know... maybe we can work on it together. Perhaps you could bring in some other professors and see if they're interested?"

"That's a good idea too. How about we work together to lay out the framework and then bring the other professors so that they can understand what we're saying. Right now, it just seems like a bunch of soundbites."

"Yeah, I can get all the resources together, like what's available for us, where we can do it, and any permission slips that may be needed for kids who are still seventeen. It doesn't have to be a movie. It could also be some form of mixed media."

"Cool. Sounds good. When do you want to meet?"

"Tonight," I said.

Her brows popped. "Oh... okay. I'm free. And you know, Max, you can call me Q. Most people think my name is a mouthful," she said, her eyes downcast almost as if she was embarrassed to say it. Her legs shifted, one going in and the other moving outward in a nervous shuffle.

"People who can't say your name just have lazy mouths. I don't have that problem."

That got her attention, and it wasn't until she brought her eyes to mine with an excited look that I realized what I said.

"Okay, and on that note, I'll go ahead and get started." She stood from where she leaned against the desk and walked toward the door.

I knew in my heart I should have apologized to her. It was a very forward statement, and I hadn't intended the double entendre... But it was out there, nonetheless. That shit was real Freudian, and I should have been ashamed of the implication. But I wasn't, if I were being honest. Nor did I apologize. I simply let her walk out the door with the thought that my mouth was definitely not lazy.

Quivina might very well end up being my brother's girl, and that in itself should've made me feel guilty for greedily coveting her. I didn't feel that either.

Chapter Eleven

MAX

I WAS at the hospital with the kids selfishly thinking about my plans later that evening. The 360Project's motivational mixer would be a fun time. Yes, the kids would love it, but there was extra incentive because I got to work on it with Quivina.

I had given myself a pass because I told myself that this was purely for work. But I knew there was a little bit more to it. I knew I was looking forward to spending time with her, and if that was all I could get because she and my brother were seeing one another, then I would take it.

"Uncle Max," Diane said in her excited voice.

"Yes, sweetheart?" I replied.

"When Mom gets back from her test, do you think I can move everything out of the way and show her my new somersault?" My sweet niece looked up at me with wide eyes.

"I don't think there's enough room, baby. But this weekend when you're at practice, how about I come and record the routine for her? I think that will work out a little bit better."

"Would you? That is a great idea, Uncle Max."

"Can I be on the recording too?" Donnie asked.

"Of course. You can show her the project you're working on in NASA camp."

With both of them smiling and turning their attention to their individual tablets as we waited, I felt the weight of their fear. It was important for them to still feel as though their mother was participating. Cami was the type of mom who was there for her kids despite how tired she was, or how daunting the task. She would weather any storm for those children. And as much as they needed it, I knew she needed it too.

I heard the wheels of the gurney coming down the hallway and knew she was coming back from her test. Thankfully, she had a private room so we were able to chill and wait for her whenever we got there too early. There were so many tests and every time we came, I noticed my sister getting more and more tired. If I didn't know God had stopped listening to me long ago, I would have been on my knees every night.

"I see you have company," the RN in penguin-covered scrubs exclaimed as she came around the corner.

In the next few seconds, I saw the gurney being wheeled in and my sister looking half-asleep and so very small underneath the covers.

"My babies," Cami said. As the orderlies moved her bed into place and locked the wheels, the nurse positioned her in the bed by raising the head. "Y'all look so cute today. Have you been giving Uncle Max a hard time?"

"No, Mommy," the pair said in unison.

I knew very well they had been giving me a run for my money and if I didn't know any better, I'd swear they were enjoying it. "No, they're not. We've been great. I even learned a couple of vegetarian recipes for Donnie. And my cooking is almost edible."

Donnie was the first to pipe up. "Not so much, but we eat it anyway."

That caused a round of laughter in the room.

I was ready to defend myself when I heard someone else enter. I turned to find Smith standing there with a twisted grin on his face. "You know you can't cook, Max." He walked over to the bed and wrapped his arm around Diane before turning to our sister. "How you feelin', sis?"

"I'm doing pretty good. I can't complain, and I'm still here. But with all of you showing up here today, I'm wondering if there's some kind of plot afoot. What are you guys up to?"

"Nothing. We just wanted to see how you were doing and lay eyes on you. FaceTime isn't as good as the real thing," I said.

Smith nodded in agreement. "Yeah, we can't come to see our sister? What, you've got a hot date tonight?"

"My mom doesn't date," Donnie interjected.

"I wish I did, especially since I have babysitters now." She was laughing, but I could tell from the stiffness in her face that she was covering up her pain and her weakness.

Smith leaned over and kissed our sister on the forehead and then came to take a seat beside me. Donnie and Diane closed in on Cami, each one of them telling her stories about their day. Smith and I didn't interrupt. They deserved all the time with their mom.

I leaned closer to my brother to ask the question I was dreading. "Hey, you free tonight?"

"Yup, I'll be home reviewing tape for the upcoming season. We're trying to get the starting lineup together before the first preseason game."

"You mind if I bring the kids over tonight? I got this work thing, and—"

"You mean you have a thing with Q? She told me you and her were putting together a program for the 360 kids. And yeah, of course I can watch them."

"Yeah, I was going to say she and I were working on a project together." I was lying. I'd had no intention of mentioning that she and I were working together on a project. I didn't know what that was about, really. Maybe it was the guilt. I already felt bad about the way I was thinking about her, the things I wanted to do with her. I wouldn't give in, though. Smith was my brother, and I had put him through enough.

"Okay. What time are you bringing them by? I'm making a pot of basil fried rice."

"Most likely around seven. It shouldn't go too late, no more than a couple of hours."

"Why? Don't come and pick them up late. Just bring some clothes with them and I'll take them to the camps tomorrow."

"You don't want me to pick you guys up from your apartment in the morning?" I asked. With Smith not driving, I didn't want them to be inconvenienced. Even though he only lived about a mile from the school.

"No, we'll take a Lyft."

"We're spending the night at Uncle Smith's house?" Diane asked the question, and I marveled at how she tracked two conversations at one time.

"Yeah, you're coming over and we're making some really good food. Then we'll all watch a movie when I'm done watching game tape."

"Oh, Uncle Max do you have a date?" Donnie trained his eyes on me and narrowed them.

"No. Nothing like that. It's a work thing. I'm working on a project with a colleague."

Even as I denied it, a rush of heat washed over me. I knew I would feel terrible later, but some things were worth the risk.

After we left the hospital, I swung by the apartment and grabbed a set of clothes and overnight bag for the kids before dropping Smith, Donnie, and Diane off at his apartment. We probably could've had the kids at my place, but they could be a handful and kind of demanding for such little people.

I gave the house a good once-over, put a couple of cans of Perrier in the refrigerator, and ordered a pizza. I thought about wine but knew that probably wouldn't be a good idea for me. I didn't want my inhibitions to drop even a millimeter. It was already going to be hard enough to be around her without letting my libido get in the way. I got my laptop from the bedroom, because we were for sure working in the living room. About five minutes early, I heard the knock on the door. I forgot she was staying with a friend in the building until she found a place. A fact that only made matters worse. But we could work together. I could be professional and not a cock-hound.

I walked over to the door and opened it without asking who it was. Very few people visited me, and since it wasn't Smith, it would have to be her. As I swung the door open, her sweet scent of lilacs and honey washed over me. I took her in. She wore a loose tee that showed shoulder skin, fitted skinny jeans with rips across the thighs, and a pair of designer flip-flops. While her attire was casual, she wrecked me. I felt my nerve endings awakening everywhere inside.

"Hello Max," she said, then gave a red lipstick-coated smile.

"Hello. Come in," I said.

I closed the door behind her after waving her in. Then I said a silent prayer, even if I knew the good Lord wasn't listening, that I could keep my hands to myself.

Chapter Twelve

MAX HAD the kind of apartment that you would expect a history professor to have. The walls were lined with bookshelves, even in the dining room. You could see evidence of his notetaking and open books on nearly every table. The only one that was cleared was the dining room table. I could only imagine it was because he was trying to clean up his act since children were at his home most every night. I laid my purse on the coffee table in front of his worn leather couch and then took a seat.

"Would you like something to drink? I have some sparkling water in the fridge." Max seemed a little stiffer than he'd been earlier in the day. He'd changed into jeans and a lightweight T-shirt that stretched over his shoulders and muscular arms. I'd never seen him in anything quite as casual, and simply put, he was gorgeous. He had a runner's physique, lean but muscular. Instead of his standard loafers, he had on blue shoes with white soles, somehow effortlessly matched to his jeans and light blue shirt. He resembled a runway model, his handsome face chiseled and distinctly masculine.

"Blah. Doesn't that stuff taste a little like Alka-Seltzer to you?" I gave him my half smile. "I didn't expect you to be so bougie."

"Bougie? I feel affronted," he said, with a playful shake of his head. "I have some regular old water if you like? Or apple juice? Those drinks a little more down to earth for you?" An uncommon smile played on his lips. I'd only ever seen it once or twice before, but it meshed well with his eyes that, at the moment, seemed to have fireworks behind them.

"I was thinking maybe wine. Or do you not drink? Because if you don't, I completely understand. But I thought since we're just casually putting this project together, maybe we could have a glass. I do understand kids live here, so if you need me to run upstairs and grab a bottle of sauvignon blanc for us—"

I realized I was babbling but hopefully, wine would calm me down. And one glass of wine wouldn't lower my inhibitions, something I needed to be worried about being alone with a man like Maxwell.

"I have wine. I just thought... Since we were technically working, I didn't want to come out with that. But if you prefer, I do have a nice petite shiraz in the kitchen. I'll open it, but you have to swear not to take advantage of me."

"Professor Wynn, I would never do anything untoward. You have my word." I held my lying hands up to my heart. Even if I wouldn't act on it, I for sure thought about it. But... Smith. Sweet Smith was Max's brother. I should probably be flogged.

"I'm gonna hold you to that. I'll be right back." He gave me a slight nod before turning and walking into the kitchen. I looked around the walls and saw pictures of so many different people in gilded frames. And while this house did look like it belonged to a history professor, it didn't quite resonate with his personality. It was as if someone else had decorated using only their perspective and none of his. His home looked like he just stayed there and didn't actually live in it.

The thought made me want to get up and wander around just to see if the books were actually something that he would read or just there for show. That made no sense, especially since most professors read quite a bit. But in my heart, I knew something was off. And it was absolutely none of my business. Especially if I was going to keep dating his brother. I liked Smith, I really did. But I hadn't felt the same type of reaction for him as I had for Max. But maybe that would come in time. Even if I'd practically been in an arranged marriage with Kenyon, eventually I'd grown to like him and then to love him. No matter that it didn't exactly yield the desired results.

I gave in and got up to walk around, looking at the pictures on the walls and the books on the shelves and even sniffing the incense lying on a buffet in the corner. The scent was sandalwood and reminded me of his aftershave.

I got to the picture sitting on the desk near the front window and had to pick it up. It was of Max and a woman with very fair skin and long, flowing hair. He was staring down at her, and I knew there was love between them. A pang of jealousy hit me from nowhere, and I had no idea why. I didn't know who that woman was, I didn't even know if they had been intimate, and further, why should that have bothered me? But it still was there, the niggling feeling fluttering around in the back of my brain and just beneath my heart.

"My ex-wife," he said, having walked into the room without my noticing.

I nearly dropped the frame on the floor. But I recovered

and set it down gently back on the desk. "I'm sorry, I didn't mean to pry. I just wanted to get a sense of who you are. Forgive me for saying so and this may be forward as well, but you are a little guarded on first meeting."

Max walked over to me and extended a hand with wine in a stemless glass. "It's fine. I'm actually kind of an open book. I like to be upfront with people, so they know where I'm coming from, so no one has to guess. It makes my life a lot easier."

"Ha. I think the world would be a better place if more people were like you." I took a sip of my wine and rolled the liquid around in my mouth, letting the light, peppery taste float over my senses. He was right, it was quite delightful. I took another small sip before stepping around him and heading back to the couch.

"So, what do you think?"

I sat down and leaned forward to set the glass on the table. Wouldn't do for me to drink that fast. I could tell the alcohol content was not for games. "It's really nice. But I think if I had two glasses you might have to walk me back upstairs. I am prone to taking a wobble when I'm tipsy." I laughed.

TMI, Quivina.

"Yeah, I think I can see that. It's a little bit of a high alcohol content. Although it takes a lot for me to get drunk. Have a very high tolerance."

Max walked across the room and took a seat on the opposite chair. I was kind of glad that he didn't sit right beside me on the couch. My body was firing off signals that I didn't quite understand. He wasn't the guy I was supposed to be interested in. Max had a bit of a mean streak, I worked with him, and for some reason, I got the impression that he had done something to Smith. The way Smith talked about the accident, the way he danced around stating what actually occurred leading up to his amputation left me wondering. But Smith would tell me in his own time. Max seemed like the type of man who had a few demons, but instead of being a turnoff, well... it was actually becoming intriguing. Except, I didn't need a mean guy or one with secrets. Shouldn't I have had enough of that?

"I do not. As a matter of fact, I only just recently started drinking again. I had almost forgotten how much I love wine."

"Was it for religious purposes?"

"No, nothing like that. My ex-husband... He just preferred that I didn't drink. And I obliged him."

"Oh, I see."

"Well, it wasn't like he forced me not to drink. He just made really strong suggestions about me being ready in the event he brought home guests. He was the type of guy who would call an hour before and say was bringing home five friends, leaving me the task of preparing dinners for seven people at the drop of a dime. He for sure kept me on my toes."

"That sounds like a fantastic marriage." He rolled his eyes, then cleared his throat as if he'd caught himself slipping. "That's probably wrong of me to say, but as a person who wasn't in a fantastic marriage either, I figure we are comrades in arms."

"I honestly don't think Kenyon meant to be such a horrible person to me. I think... I think I was so eager to please him that I forgot about what I needed. And I never made my feelings a priority. I just allowed myself to be kind of an ornament. That part was on me."

"I get that. I think my problem with my wife... my ex-wife, was just that I never loved her enough. I married her because that's what I was supposed to do. I was supposed to graduate from college, get a good job, meet the woman of my dreams, and then marry her and have a bunch of babies. But it didn't happen. I missed a step. Sometimes you don't know what your dreams are, so you reach for the wrong thing." As he said the words, he gazed off as if he was realizing something for the very first time. "I'm sorry, we're supposed to be working on this project of ours. Not reminiscing on all our past failures."

"Well, that was my bad. I brought it up and took us down the dark path."

"It's all good. It doesn't hurt anymore, so I can finally talk about it. But yours is more recent, so I understand if you need to talk about it."

Silence stretched between us as I figured out what to say next.

"Did you bring your laptop?" he asked, mercifully breaking the silence between us.

"Yeah, I did." I lifted my bag from the coffee table and brought it closer to me. I pulled out my tablet, which was small enough to carry in my purse and big enough for me to work on without straining my eyes. I lifted the tablet and shook it in his direction. "Always prepared. Did you email what you have over to me already?"

"Yeah, you should have it." Max set his wine down on the hardwood floor beside his chair and went to retrieve a notepad and a laptop.

When he came back, we started work. We laid out what we thought would be a good format for biweekly sessions in the theater consisting of documentaries, biographies, and lectures on all of the great minority and otherwise disenfranchised contributors to arts and sciences.

Attendance would afford extra credit for any coursework in 360Project where the students were struggling. All they would have to do is come in for two hours and be engaged with the presentation for the night. It was brilliant, because not only did it offer them a leg up in course-work where they would potentially struggle, it would also show them that despite a person's inherent disadvantages, there were still opportunities for them if they applied themselves.

It took about three hours to get the plan laid out and documented. We had included suggestions from all of the primary subjects of 360Project. Math, English, science, and history were all represented. The only thing missing was public speaking, which was also a program requirement, but with only four weeks of sessions, we decided to only use the major subjects. Of course we would need to discuss it with the other professors and faculty team members to make sure it was a feasible program, but honestly by the time were done, I was amazed we'd just thought it up earlier that afternoon.

"Well done," I said. "We make a great team. I'm actually really proud of this." I had long since finished my glass of wine and somehow magically the glass had refilled and I finished that too. I wasn't tipsy, though, so it was okay. And it did help me calm down and eased some of the tension.

"Yeah, I think so too. This is really going to work. Your idea was wonderful, and I can't believe we hadn't thought of something like this before. I'll be sure that you get the credit due from the dean of my school, as well as the dean of yours. And just so you know, you make a great addition to the staff."

"Thank you so much for saying that. You know I haven't worked since I got married. And that was a long time ago. I was wondering if I had lost my edge. You know that burning desire to change the world that you have right when you graduate and give your dissertation? I haven't felt that type of passion in a very long time. I wondered if it was even still there."

"I think we all wonder that from time to time, Quivina. It's not just you."

I looked up at him and caught his eyes trained on me. It was as if he was observing me and trying to figure out where I was coming from.

"I know. Every now and again people have moments of doubt. But mine wasn't that. For years, my husband reminded me that I wouldn't be able to make it without him. After so long, I began to wonder if that was true."

"He was wrong. I hardly even know you, and I know he was dead wrong. People like you don't lose their spark. It had to always be there... always right there with you just beneath the surface waiting for the perfect moment to shine."

I was so taken aback by his kind words, I didn't know what to say. I just sat there, my eyes locked on his. He looked at me as if he saw the entire world inside me. I'd never, ever been looked at like he was staring at me. And as stupid as it sounds, in that moment, he made me feel more special than I ever had in my entire life.

"I... I'm sorry. That was probably too much. Let's blame it on the wine," he said, breaking the gaze that had probably gone on for too long.

"It-it's okay. I appreciate your words. Even if you're just being nice." A warmth burned somewhere deep that I wasn't ready to acknowledge. His ability to make me feel so incredibly important and valued in such a short time was hard to accept. His kindness made me feel uneasy, yet simultaneously completely treasured.

"No. I'm not just being nice. The one thing I have going for me is that I am an excellent judge of character. I can always tell how great someone is. And you, Quivina Adedeji, seem pretty great to me." He stood up and took the glass from in front of me and went back into the kitchen.

I glanced down at my watch and realized it was nearly eleven p.m. And we were done with our work. I should've been collecting my things and getting ready to leave. But he hadn't asked me to leave, nor I did want to go. My thoughts drifted back to Nell telling me that I had the ability to choose. I decided at that moment that if he didn't ask me to leave, then I would stay.

I heard his footsteps and my heart sped up again. It was the damnedest thing, but everything Max did seemed so very passionate and intense. Everything with him felt so important, like anything we said to one another would become this critical piece of history.

I was surprised to see that he didn't have our wine glasses in his hands. I was even more surprised when he didn't come back across the room. He just stood there, his eyes clouded over. This Max was the one I'd met in the parking lot that day. Whatever happened in the minutes between him going into the kitchen and returning to the living room seemed to form a sheet of ice over his surface. Was it even possible for someone to change so completely in such a minuscule period of time?

"This has been so much fun, Quivina. But it's getting late. It's a school night after all."

Obviously, I had been wrong. Maybe I was just so unfamiliar with the laws of attraction that I couldn't even recognize them anymore. "I completely understand. And I had a good time. Thank you for the wine." I tried to keep my voice cool as I closed my tablet and slid it back into my bag before placing the bag on my shoulder. I stood to leave. "I guess I'll see you in school tomorrow." I gave him a smile, the best one I could fake, then brushed past him to get the door. As our shoulders grazed one another's, the pulse of an electric charge ran through me. Though I wanted to stop, I had to keep moving. I had to get out of there before I said or did something stupid.

I could hear Max walking behind me across the hard-wood floor. Three urgent steps and he was nearly in front of me, his hand reaching for the door before I could make it there. He opened it but not wide enough for me to leave. His chest was against my back as I stood in the narrow space between his hard body and escape. I could feel his shallow breaths on my neck and smell his earthy scent—the sultry combination threatened to consume me. I clutched my hands together in an effort to control the tidal wave of desire that whirled inside me.

"Are you going to let me go, Max?" The question came out in a whisper. This hardly recognizable version of myself was speaking to someone I longed to have hold me captive.

"I am... I will... let you go," he said, his warm breath on my neck like a sensual caress.

And then it was over.

"Good night, Quivina." He slowly pulled the door open and let me out.

"Good night, Max." I didn't look back at him, mostly because I didn't know what to expect. I didn't know why, but I felt like the momentary yet deeply passionate flash of intimacy that had transpired had been the last time for us. Some unspoken yet devastating end of us.

When I made it back to Nell's apartment, I attempted to explain my about-face with someone who'd taken me through too many emotions to be healthy in such a short time.

"With the brother who likes me, there's no magic. But with the off-limits brother there's all the magic in the world.

I can't win for losing. Max has the making of toxic, and right now, I don't need that shit in my life. So, maybe it's best if I stop seeing both of them."

Nell was already in her *Buffy the Vampire Slayer* PJs. "Oh girl, I'm so sorry. Come sit down." She patted the cushion next to her, which had become our wine-and-popcorn or wine-and-Rice-Krispies-Treat positioning.

I walked over, even though I didn't want any more wine, and took the proffered seat. "Maybe you've spent too much time focusing on the boys since you started this journey to find yourself. And so what if you don't know which of them you like... You aren't stuck with either of them. Just focus on what you need and who you see yourself becoming."

I sat back on the couch and considered that. Since I'd married Kenyon, I longed for a job and the freedom to be myself. Now that it was happening just that way, I was focused on the wrong thing... on men instead of what I needed. I glanced over at Nell, who propped her head up with her hand and leaned over the arm of the couch.

"You know what? You're absolutely right. That's why you're my bestie. Because you're brilliant. Now go to bed. You look like you're about to fall over," I said.

As I made my way to my own bed, I saw my night with Max exactly for what it was—the start of a really great project for some kids who needed a new reality. That was the part I loved.

The rest would wait until I had what I needed. Myself.

Chapter Thirteen

MAX

I DON'T KNOW what burned me up the most. The fact that after our night of planning, Quivina and I only communicated via email or that the next time I saw her again was on the first day of 360Project being kissed by my brother. It wasn't anything scandalous. She parked her car, and he got out of the passenger side, walked around to her, and leaned in to kiss her on the cheek.

Smith was a goddamned fool, because if I were dating her, I would have kissed her on the mouth. I pulled my messenger bag onto my shoulder and stalked toward the school, careful to walk the long way around to avoid the happy couple. I really was being a bastard. None of it was either of their faults. Quivina had joined a dating app, like any normal single person. Smith had responded to her when he saw her beautiful face, like any other man would have done when confronted with such beauty.

My head understood all of it perfectly. It was the rest of me—my yearning soul and my longing heart, in particular—

that was having no part of that. Both wanted Quivina, and her absence for the last few days only seemed to amplify the desire.

I made it to my office and began my slow brew, pouring freshly ground coffee beans into the decanter, filling it with filtered water, and starting my makeshift double-boiler method of brewing. It took a while to get to the desired strength, but I loved the flavor. If a person wanted something enough, I didn't think having to wait should be a deterrent.

By the time I was done setting up the coffee, my mind drifted back to Quivina. I contemplated everything from how much time she and Smith were spending together to whether or not they were falling in love. Shit, there was obviously no distracting me that morning. With Quivina living in my building, he would stop by and say hello to me and the kids before heading home for the night. The shit was driving me to distraction. It was maddening. Based on his conversations with me, they had been on a date every night, to the point where I wondered how she was getting any work done at all. But she kept on producing.

With each passing day, I felt more and more infuriated. Not at Smith, because he was just trying to live his best life. Maybe I was angry with myself, because I had met her first, after all. If I hadn't been in such a rush that day in the parking lot, maybe I could've asked her out on a date. Perhaps if I'd just known how to take care of myself as much as I tried to care for others, I would have at least seen the opportunity.

Thankfully, classes had started for 360Project. I was getting into my groove, learning all about the new students and about everything they wanted from a college education. And we had a great response to our first Inspiration Alley event, which was what we ended up titling the movie nights. The students had even set up props to make the theater look like an alley from Detroit streets.

Many professors were joining in, eager to include their first moment of discovery, be it a significant scholar who had opened their eyes to their chosen subject matter or something a bit closer to home, like a teacher who introduced them to their career then encouraged them to go for it. It had turned out better than I'd expected. Quivina was an asset, which is what I would be writing up in her performance review to the dean of her school. Just because she wasn't interested in me romantically didn't mean I would sabotage her career. There was nothing worse than toxic masculinity, and far too much of it already existed in academia.

The knock on the door pulled me from my thoughts. "Yup," I called out, not fully up to people-ing just yet.

"It's me." Smith stuck his head inside the room. "You didn't hear me calling you outside?"

"Huh? Um, no," I turned away from what I'd been working on to give my brother my full attention. He didn't need to know I was a bit pissy about his relationship... even though I was very much perturbed by it all. We dapped one another up, and I nodded over to a chair, offering him a seat. "What's good?"

"Nothing, man. Just came over to say hi. I haven't seen much of you in a few days and thought I should check in. How are the littles?"

I couldn't help but smile. Donnie was being as militant as ever in his meat strike, and Lady Di was running the house with her iron fist wrapped in a velvet glove. Neither of them knew how much of a tightrope they had me walking.

"Same. I'm terrified." The laughter spilled over as soon as I said the words.

"You'll be all right. Just try to meet their demands and they usually leave you alone."

"Agreed. On a serious note, Cami may be coming home next week. I'm thinking she should come to my place until she gets her strength back."

Smith winced, and I knew what he was getting at. "You tell her that yet?"

"No... I was kinda hoping you would. She has a soft spot for you... since you're the baby."

"You want me to tell that woman she can't go to her house after she finally gets out of the hospital? Shit, man. You must be as crazy as you look."

"I just think it's for the best. She's going to be weak, and I don't want to leave that on the kids." He had a point, though. I scrubbed my hand over my face, thinking over the confrontation.

"That may very well be, but I still think we should ask her what she wants first. It may be easier to walk her into it backwards."

"In other words, you're scared too?"

"Basically." Smith locked his fingers behind his neck and rolled his eyes. "She likes to do things on her own. I don't want to take that away from her too. She's had a rough couple of years... his deployment and their separation, and trying to get the kids adjusted to their new life. Then she got sick..."

"Fine. I'll go talk to her tonight. But you pick the kids up from school. I'm not walking them into a war zone."

Smith adjusted his big body in the chair. He was a couple of sizes too big for it, bulky with muscle. "Yeah, I can do that. You sure you don't want to wait? She may ask you herself."

"It's best to take the bull by the horns. Seems like you've been pretty busy with Quivina, so just let me know if you won't have the time." I couldn't help the jab, and I realized the words came out a bit more snarky than I wanted. Real men didn't snark, did they? Whether I intended to or not, my iciness filled the room. I felt it radiating from my body.

Smith's brows rose right around the time the chilled air hit him. "Wow, we're going there? She's cool, that's all. I'm reintroducing her to Detroit. And I'm pretty sure I don't have to explain myself. I promise not to break her precious brain. She'll still be able to teach kids after walking on the wild side, Max." His voice was both amused and terse.

"Well, I wasn't saying all that... Calm your nerves. I'm just messing with you," I covered, lying through my teeth. I was absolutely not *just messing with him*, I was verbally sparring, even though it was the last thing I should have been doing.

"Whatever, man. I'm not bothered by that. And if you must know, Q is on a journey to the new her. So, we're just friends. I've been taking her exploring, and she's trying to figure it all out."

"That's cool. I wish y'all the best. It's none of my business what you two do." I shrugged my shoulders, doing my best to play nonchalant. And failing at it.

"Would you stop it, man." Smith let out a sigh and stood. "Something seems a little off with you. I'm not sure what it is, and I don't even know if I wanna know, but if you're angry with me for some reason, you should just come out with it."

"Not angry, just making an observation."

"You do know I've known you most of my life, don't you? I can tell when you're pissy. But I'm not going to beg you to tell me what's wrong. You can talk whenever you're ready."

"Pissy?"

Smith turned and headed for the door, his shoulders set tensely as he walked. "Like I said, whatever. I'll go over to your place later to grab that tie I loaned you. Call the guard and have him let me in." Smith was on the other side of the door before the sentence finished. I watched as it clicked into its frame after Smith left it swinging.

"All right," I said to no one at all. I had been weird. I shouldn't have brought her up, nor their dates or the frequency of them. I was being a dick. The worst thing about being a prick was figuring out how to stop yourself from being one.

By the time I got to class, I was in no better mood.

"Just because you don't acknowledge something doesn't mean it's not real." I stopped after my statement and glanced around the lecture hall to find wide-eyed stares. It was a good feeling, to captivate an audience. I had just expanded the minds of my freshman students exponentially. Or they were bored to death. "For my generation, it was one of those moments that would forever stand out in our memories. For my parents, that would have been the assassinations of President John F. Kennedy and Dr. Martin Luther King. I will certainly never forget this horrible tragedy. Most of us piled around a television in various auditoriums and gymnasiums across these United States to watch the first teacher go up into outer space, and damn, we were so excited. I was nine years old. Seventy-three seconds into the launch, with our collective hearts and minds open, young and hopeful, we watched seven souls blown into oblivion. No one explained what happened for months," I explained with a sigh. "In fact, I went home and made dinner. My mother was working, and we were a generation of latchkey kids, so who would we talk to anyway? We should have acknowledged our pain, though, because on January 28, 1986, we all lost our trust."

A young man's hand shot up in the back. Pointing to him, I gave him a nod. "Yes?"

"Professor Wynn, is that why Baby Boomers don't trust like anything, even when they have evidential proof?"

Oh yeah, I was really off because hearing my generation referred to as Boomers in that moment felt like someone had put me on a spit and rotated me over an open flame. "We are not Boomers. We are Generation X. We invented hip-hop and Napster. You'll also hear us called the Sandwich Generation, because we take care of everyone, yet no one knows who we are," I said. Too forcefully because I could almost see the kids mentally retreating. Instead of continuing, I just shook my head. "So, yeah. We don't have a lot of trust in others. In fact, to help you learn the differences in the generations, I want everyone to write me a three-page essay on the inherent similarities and unique differences between Baby Boomers, Gen X, Millennials, and your own generation, Gen Z."

Collective grumbles erupted around the classroom. Then another hand rose in the back of the hall. This time, it was a young woman with a mane of curly hair. I gave her a nod and acknowledged her question. "We already have a paper due this week, so can we push this one off just a little?"

"Good question, but no. I need you to do your Challenger paper and then the generational essay. Does anyone know why it's important to learn about people outside of your own culture and time?"

No one raised a hand.

"It's important because that, my friends, is history, and knowing where you've been will help you see where you are going. It will also, hopefully, prevent you from making the same mistakes as those before us." I glanced around the room once more. No one was happy with me. But if they learned something, it would all be worthwhile. "All right, unless there are questions, we can adjourn for the day. If any of you need help, reach out to me for an appointment. And not the day before the papers are due. Understood, guys?" I said.

Half of them were already out of their seats by the time the ripple of "Yes, Professor," sounded out. Oh well. I'd make it up to them by giving anyone who completed the impromptu assignment extra credit.

I was putting my tablet in my messenger bag before I heard her voice. "Max," she said, on approach, her heels clicking against the ceramic tile of Old Main, the historic original building for Southeastern Michigan University.

I looked up at the same time the scent of honey and lilacs enveloped me, and I had to lean forward and place my palms on the desk to prevent myself from reaching for her. "Quivina." I had intended to say more, but my throat was suddenly constricted, mouth dry from one glance in her direction.

"That is one surefire way to make them love history. Drown them in it. I'm being sarcastic, by the way."

I cleared my throat and tried to speak. "Very funny. Kids react positively to responsibilities. Even if it's more work. Now," I said, returning my attention to packing my bag and very thankful my voice didn't crack like a pubescent kid's, "I'm pretty sure you didn't just come over here to be my proctor. What's up?"

"Email is down again," she said with a smile. "At least I got my steps in today. I just wanted to let you know the props are in and the caterer is set for next Wednesday. We are also at eighty-five percent in student participation. I'd say this is a success."

"That's good. We should have a full house, then."

"Yeah, we should. Well, um... I haven't seen you for a few days." She looked down at the floor before licking full, red-colored lips. I loved that fucking lipstick. When she brought her eyes back up to mine, peering up at me from beneath half-lowered lids, I felt the stirring before I could help it. "I thought you were avoiding me."

"No. Just busy." My voice was clipped, but I was semi-hard in cotton twill. If she licked her lips one more time, I was going to go full-on teenage boy, and that was not a good look in front of my brother's girl.

"Oh, yeah... I get that. Kids, your sister... You have a challenging schedule..."

"I do. But, um, if you don't mind, I'm going to head out. I have to meet one of our students at the library to review an assignment."

"Certainly... I'm sorry. I just barged in on you." She turned and started from the room. "See you later." Quivina tossed a backward glance and a wave over her shoulder.

I watched her walk away and got the full-on effect of her curves as she sauntered down the hall. The pencil skirt and high heels were more of a distraction than her mouth.

I didn't need to look down to see that my pants were having a hard time concealing my lecherous cock, like a fucking perv.

"Goddammit," I whispered under my breath. It was bad enough I'd been waking to thoughts of her, her short locks against my pillow, her mouth in an O as I toiled away above her, and her thighs on my shoulders. Perverse. That's what I was. Hopelessly gone on a woman who did not like me, but my brother. How uncomfortable would holidays get now? They were already a fucking mess.

I took my seat and realized, if I never had before, I was in deep fucking trouble.

Chapter Fourteen

QUIVINA

SINCE THE AFTERNOON had been glorious, I decided to make it doubly screwed-up and call my father. He had been avoiding me too. What was it with men deciding they were done with me?

I sat in my car and held the phone up to my ear, waiting on him to answer. It rang twice before I heard his monotone voice.

"Hello?"

"Hello, Baba. How are you?

My words were greeted with silence, the sound of something with Nigerian actors in the background. He had taken to watching our movies on YouTube a couple of years ago and had even bought a smart TV to stream them to it so he could comfortably watch. It was the only bit of technology he'd adopted. "Daughter, how are you?" he asked.

I let out my held breath and tried not to let the sound carry over the cell. "I'm okay. I just wanted to give you a call."

I could hear him sit up on the leather furniture that had been around since I was a teen. I knew he was smoking his pipe and drinking tea, rather the Nigerian version of it, which was what he always did when he watched his films and TV shows. "I am doing as well as can be expected. Your uncle though... he is unwell. Tunji has been in his bed for two weeks. Can you believe it?"

Typical of him to ignore the fact that he'd practically turned me out on the street. "That's too bad. Was he seen by a doctor?"

"Tomorrow. He can hardly get himself out of bed."

"Will you go home to see him?" My father hadn't been home for more than a decade. The last time he'd gone, Kenyon had taken him. It had been a father-and-son-he-never-had journey. "It would probably do his heart good to see you." Maybe it would do my father some good too.

"No, no. I will be embarrassed to see my family without my son-in-law."

Silence resumed. I didn't know what to say. Should I have offered to go along with him? Even though the comment was a slap in my face? I cleared my throat and tried to resume. "Well, I hope he gets better soon."

"I'm sure he'll be fine," he said, despite my Uncle Tunji being seventy-seven. "I'm glad you called, though. It's almost time for the summer party. You can come and bring some of your friends. Not the lesbian. And it's not a date thing."

I felt steam coming off my neck even though I was in my air-conditioned car. I hated the way he talked about Nell. And even more that he would dictate who I could and couldn't bring. "Nell is my friend, Baba. And anyway, I thought you weren't having it this year since my... my breakup."

"Don't be silly. It's the weekend after next. I've called the caterer and have them coming to set up the tent."

The call had been more than I expected, and I was happy we were on speaking terms, even if the ground was still shaky, but I had to know. "Did you invite Kenyon?" More silence... after a moment I couldn't take it anymore, even if I knew the answer. "Baba?"

"Yes. He is like a son to me. Of course, I asked him."

What do you do with that? I almost hung up, but our tenuous relationship probably wouldn't withstand an abrupt disconnect. "Fine." I knew my voice was clipped but it was the best I could do.

"Two weeks from Saturday. I'll see you then. Mo nife re."

"Love you too," I said.

The call ended, and I just held the phone for a moment, remembering all the times he picked me up after I fell off my bike. Then there were the other times, after my mother died, when it was my turn to pick him up. I wondered if we'd ever get back there.

I drove home and made my way up to Nell's. When I stepped into the apartment, I could smell the orange clove incense burning before I rounded the corner to the living room from the entryway. A low humming met my ears, and I looked first to the window to see if Alexa was playing some song.

When I turned back, I saw legs and arms, and two naked bodies intertwined in what could only be described as the throes of ecstasy. My audible gasp made both Nell and a very embarrassed lady of Asian descent jump and scramble for whatever was next to them—which turned out to be a throw with the saying *If you can read this, I'm watching Hallmark movies.*

Nell's unidentified girlfriend shrieked. I turned and bolted, the only thing I could think to do, then plastered myself against the wall in the entryway. "I'm so sorry!" I yelled out.

"I thought you were going on a date?" Nell's voice had a hint of annoyance steeped with embarrassment.

"It's tomorrow. I should have told you. I'm so sorry."

"It's okay. Can you just give us a minute to get decent?"

"Yes… I can. I'm so so sorry," I said again. I must have sounded like an idiot. I'd never walked in on anyone having sex before. I was so embarrassed and… frankly, I was jealous. I saw no sign of what Nell was doing to that woman in my future.

"It's all right, and please, stop saying you're sorry. No harm done… but Trinity's clothes are in the hallway… so if you could…" They were shuffling around and rushing about on the other side of the wall.

I looked down and found that I was standing on a crisp white shirt that looked too expensive to be strewn on the floor. A black lacy bra was not too far from the shirt. "Oh… right. You know what, I'll be back in a few hours. Is that okay, or do you need me—"

"No, girl. A few hours is fine. See you then."

I wasn't a mind reader, but I knew when I was being shooed away. "Okay. Nice to meet you, Trinity." It took me no more than thirty seconds to get out of there. Shit. I pulled the door closed behind me and leaned against it, relieved that most of the discomfort was over. I heard their giggles from the other side of the door, and I had to let out one of my own.

What would I do with myself for two hours?

"Who is it?" he said.

Well, I hadn't wanted to leave the building. I was tired, and after a draining day with my call to my father, I'd decided maybe I could seek a momentary respite at Max's place. We were friendly, after all. "It's Quivina."

Besides, the kids would be there so there was no way anything crazy would happen.

That was until he opened the door. Max stood there in a pair of Nike running pants and that's it. My thirsty eyes drank him in, roving over every inch of his naked torso with fine hairs peppering his chest. His body was glistening like he'd been running. A light sweat was on his brow. "Everything okay?" He licked his lips and looked at me expectantly.

"Yeah... yeah." I tried to gather myself. "I need somewhere to go for a little bit. I um... I walked in on my friend, and she has company so..."

Max smiled. I swear, every time he did that my heart clenched in my chest. "Oh... you guys need a sock method."

"I don't need that. God, I probably won't need a sock method for another century or so." I glanced over at him, hoping he caught my effort at humor.

Sadly, he didn't seem to. His brows rose to the ceiling. "Oh... well, you can chill here if you want."

What the hell was I doing? I was intruding on this man in his private time and I was a lot of things, but not rude.

"I am so sorry." I ran my hand over my skirt to get rid of the moisture. Shit, I was actually a teenager again. "I should have called first. You're busy. I can just go to a coffee house or something for a few hours."

"No... don't do that. You're here. I'm not busy. Just finished a run on the treadmill. Come on in. I can get you something to eat or drink?" While it was a statement, he asked it—as if questioning what I needed.

"Okay. I really don't want to put you out.'"

"Come in, Quivina. I don't mind." He stepped aside and waved his hand, beckoning me into his apartment.

"Thank you." I walked inside. His scent of the sea and a hint of masculine energy washed over me as I passed him.

I heard the lock click and footfalls behind me as we made our way into his apartment. I hadn't noticed how much bigger it was than Nell's until that moment. I walked over and practically fell onto his comfortable leather sofa. He was staring at me, and I wondered what was running through his mind. The look in his eyes reminded me of the most complicated math equations, the ones that had answers that spread into infinity.

"I was going to get you something to drink?" he asked. I was thankful for his words because I could have lived in the deep expanse of his captive gaze.

"I think I need it, after all. The drink..." I said. An errant giggle escaped me unexpectedly. "You know, between my dad inviting my ex-husband to his annual barbecue and walking in on my best friend with her lover fanned out on the sofa, I think something a little stronger than water is warranted. Right?"

His mouth twisted into a sly grin. "Oh yeah. Maybe some whiskey? Or do you like whiskey?" He ran a hand up a corded forearm, and I had to bite back a moan. I'd always liked when men had a dusting of hair over their arms, and interestingly long fingers. Max took it to a new level, his thick silver rings on his index and middle fingers gleaming in my direction.

"Whiskey sounds like the right prescription." I glanced down and moved my purse from one side to the other, hoping I didn't look too nervous. I was staring at him like a hungry dog looked at a T-bone. If I'd never admitted it to myself before, I wanted Maxwell Wynn. Oh Lord, I was in trouble.

"I'd better put a shirt on. I wasn't expecting company, so…"

His voice brought my reluctant gaze back to him. My mind screeched, *no, don't put a shirt on.* "Okay. If you tell me where things are, I can make our drinks?"

"The whiskey is in the cabinet over the sink. You know, out of reach from the kids. Glasses are on the minibar in the dining room. I'll be right back." Max gave me a nod before leaving the room.

I let out a long breath. Must have been holding it for a while. Pitiful. I made my way into the dining room and found a bar in the corner. He really did have a different kind of style than I would have expected. I took two highball glasses from the bar and entered the kitchen through a swiveling door. As I went through, I left the door to the tiny space open, It was hard enough being in his apartment, let alone getting closed in his narrow kitchen when his big body took up so much room.

The whiskey, labeled as Motor City Gas, was right where he said it would be. I had to jump a bit to reach the cabinet myself. Pulling it down, I uncorked it and inhaled the woodsy oak scent inherent to most good whiskey. My father preferred scotch, but he used to tell me all about scents and notes, the impact they have on your tastebuds. Funny the things you keep with you through adulthood. He'd meant for me to know how to entertain people at my husband's dinner parties, always looking ahead to my future husband even before I'd known what he was doing.

"I see you found it." Max's voice drifted into my thoughts. He really was a silent walker, despite his height and mass.

"I did." I filled the two glasses to just above the ice

cubes. "I didn't know if you took yours neat... so I made it like mine instead." I handed him the glass.

"This is fine," he said.

I was thinking we should go back to the living room, but he stood there, blocking my path. His kitchen had a wall to see through to the dining room, kind of a serving window, and the setting sun shined in over his handsomeness, brown eyes lit with more playfulness than I'd ever seen on his face. I took a sip of my drink, allowing the heat to run over my senses. I hoped it would dull whatever was going on inside me.

"It's good." I ran my tongue over my lips to gather up the last tastes of the spicy drink.

"One of my favorites. I don't drink that often, so when I do, I like to enjoy it." His eyes dropped from mine to wander over me before he looked down at his glass and placed it on the counter. "So, uh... you wanna talk about your day? You seem a little worse for the wear."

"You talk like a historian," I jabbed, looking down at my own glass and swirling the contents.

"And you're always dressed up. Maybe we both belong in other times," he said.

"How so?"

"Well, I always dig through African American history, and back in the day," he said, pulling up air quotes, "sisters were always well dressed for photos. I mean from the 1800s to the late 60s, they were damn near regal. I love that. I think we kind of started sliding away from that somewhere around the hip-hop timeline."

"You almost sound like women shouldn't be wearing pants," I said.

Max waved a hand in my direction. "Nah, that's not it. It was just this sense of pride down to the way they looked at the camera. You know what I mean?"

"I do. I guess I just never thought of it. You know, when I look at women dressed in traditional Nigerian dress, I'm so moved. I mean, God, they possess a power that I can't even put into words. I don't know if I could ever be as strong."

Max shook his head. "Oh, your strength shows. The first day I met you, I almost bowed. You looked at me like I was there to park your car." He let go of a gentle chuckle.

"I never apologized for blocking you in. I am so sorry about that. I was just having a bad day. I was arguing with my father and—"

"I wasn't exactly friendly either..."

"But then you let me park in your spot. That was nice."

"It was the least I could do."

"Well, thank you for that."

"You're welcome. But I didn't finish telling you. I gave you the spot because I felt damn near arrested by your presence. You know what I mean. Shit, I must sound a little crazy. But, if I hadn't been in a rush, I would have taken those bags up for you. I guess I should apologize for my behavior too. I was trying to get to my sister and had to drop my niece off. I was having a bit of a day myself."

"I appreciated the gesture, but given the circumstances, I wasn't exactly in the best place either. I guess, given the way we treated one another, it's a miracle we've made it this far."

"I guess so." Max grabbed his drink and then shook the glass in the direction of the door. "Let's go have a seat. You're lucky, you know. You don't have to be subjected to my terrible cooking with the kids at Pronto's. I mean, Smith's."

"Oh, I know his nickname," I said, following him back to the living room.

Max was silent for a moment. He walked to the sofa, then as if he changed his mind, he walked over to the chair opposite the couch. "That's right. You two seem to be getting close."

I took another sip and slid into my seat. "We're great friends," I said, aware that I put a bit too much emphasis on the word *friends*. "I mean, we share a lot of personal truths."

"I see. Glad you guys are hitting it off." Max took a drink from his glass and leaned back into the chair. I didn't know why, but it almost felt as if he were coming to terms with something.

"Yeah, we are..." I swished my drink again, staring down into the mahogany liquid and pondering whether I even had the right to say what was actually on my mind. But fuck it. "I wish I could say the same for his brother." I looked up from my glass and stared directly at him.

The sunlight cascaded in, shards of light created by the windowpane showing all the microscopic dust particles, making it easier to see what hadn't been visible before. Max's face was inanimate, his expression concealed behind a mask. Apparently, not even the sun could show everything.

"I like you," he said, lips barely parting as he pushed the words out.

"Do you? I think you tolerate me because I'm on your team. Because it's the right thing to do." Even as I said the words, I knew I wasn't speaking all of my truth. I wanted him to dispute me and tell me how he liked me. No, even that wasn't it. I wanted him to tell me he desired me. Like... like I desired him. More than Smith. I enjoyed our time together, but there was a chemistry with Max. Something that made me want to capture him, like a firefly at dusk.

"I always do the right thing, Quivina."

"Always? You never do anything wrong?"

Max ran a hand over the back of his neck, a sheepish look on his face. "Three weeks ago, I would have told you yes. Now... well, now I realize if I wanted something... or someone bad enough, I would do just about anything. Whether right or wrong."

All the air sucked out of the room as he said the words, and I clenched my thighs together in an effort to extinguish and flames that lapped at my flesh. "What about speeding down the street in the middle of the night when no one is out?" I asked weakly in a lame attempt to right our friendly conversation.

"I make it a point to never be in a rush. Especially behind the wheel."

"How about..." I glanced around the room, thinking of other bad things that were so small, so inconsequential, that most people did them. "Leave the shopping cart in the middle of the parking lot?"

"Absolutely not. Buggies take off in the wind and could chip the paint off people's cars."

"Well, that's almost boring, Max."

"If you make a practice of doing bad shit, it's a gateway to other bad shit. That's how people end up hurt." Max drank down the rest of his drink and stood. "Ready for another?"

"Uh..." I glanced down. I was still only halfway done. "No. I'm good for now."

"Okay. I promise, I won't get drunk and start in on historical trivia. I've learned over the years, people hate that."

"Well, thank you! I'd fail," I said. Max left to get another pour.

I rose and started around the room again, that feeling back that most of the things were just not quite him. I heard him return a few moments later. "You didn't decorate this place, did you?" I asked, turning to face him and rotating my finger in the air.

"No. My ex-wife decorated. She was all about hardwood

and drapes. I'm more of a blinds and mixed-material guy. She was more conservative than I am."

"You mean there is a person on the planet more conservative than you?"

He laughed at that, walking over to stand in front of me. He pointed at the wall behind me. "See that?"

I turned to look. He was pointing to a metal mirror with spikes all around it, in alternating directions. The formation resembled a nest of sorts. It was gorgeous and stood out. "That's edgy."

"It's the only thing in this entire room that I picked out. I brought it home one day, and Renee, my ex, she put it in the back linen closet. When she left, she didn't want anything, so I kept all this. But that," he said, taking a sip of his fresh drink, "came out of the closet as soon as the divorce was final."

"How long ago?"

"Five years ago. You?"

"My divorce was final a little under a year ago. But he'd been living with his girlfriend for about three years before then."

"Ah, yours was another woman? Mine was my own fault. I never should have married her in the first place. But we've been down this road before. You've had enough trauma in your evening."

"I have. I think I need a pick-me-up." A dry chuckle escaped and filled the distance between us.

Max set the glass down on the bookshelf and leaned against it. "I don't know for sure if you came to the right place for that. I'm not one who people usually ask to make them feel better. I am the reliable one, though. I'll always open the door when you need shelter." Max smiled down at me.

I looked up to him, then remembered my drink in my

hand. I drank it down as if summoning strength I knew I would need. "I don't know about all that. You seem more than reliable. You seem like you could make someone feel better."

I stared at him. The brother I should not be getting closer to. I should want the one I'd seemed to place in the friend zone. I should want the one who was into me and not the one I couldn't quite get a read on. I should focus on myself and not on men. So many things ran through my mind which were rational, which got in the way of my journey to self. Maybe I was just horny, or jealous of everyone who was able to jump past the hurdle of themselves to get what they wanted. I wanted that feeling—the one Nell and so many others had who were single and not trapped by their conventional roles of what women should be. I wanted all of it, and I wanted Max.

I stepped into him, inhaling the sexy scent of the fresh ocean and whiskey, but sharp and spicy, awakening my senses. I wrapped my arm around him, blinking up into his eyes.

"Quivina... I don't know what's happening, but I should stop right here. My brother—"

"Max, your brother and I are friends. We haven't made it this far... we talked about taking it slow and if it never happened, that would be fine. I already told him I'm conflicted and don't know what I want. The only thing I didn't share with him was the source of my conflict... Because it's you."

Max stepped back a bit, blinking down at me like he was working out the Pythagorean theorem. "You told him all that?"

"I did. We agreed that we could hang out while I tried new things... he said he wanted to help me."

"Why didn't he mention it to me?"

It was my turn to work out equations in my head. "Why would he do that?" I asked, voice still in a whisper. I stepped forward again, aware that I was being more forward than I'd ever been in my life. "So Max, I'm here asking you... do you like me?" God, I sounded like an immature schoolgirl.

Max's brows knitted and he took a step forward, his body so close to mine but not touching me. I breathed him in once more, his scent intoxicating.

"How about I show you how much I like you?" he asked.

In another step, he backed me against the bookshelf. I heard the ornaments on top of it clink. His arms went around my waist, and he hovered. I realized in an instant, with his hard body pressed against me and our hearts beating against one another behind our ribcages, he was waiting for me. I nodded, locking my arm around his waist again, trying to brace myself for the tidal wave of arousal coming at me like a locomotive.

It was truly all he was waiting for because the moment I motioned, he came for me. Gathering me in his arms, he leaned down and took my mouth. The taste of him, his hungry exploration of my mouth, his hands trapping me between his body and the cool wood behind me, overtook me. I lifted my legs, wrapping them around his body.

The sound of my glass clattering to the floor echoed in my ears along with the rush of blood. I was so into him, his hand lifting me up and pinning me in place, then the slow press of his palms all the way down my sides to my ass. He gripped me so tight, I felt as if we were melding together.

We wouldn't let one another break for air, greedily taking from one another, our mouths fused together, and our bodies locked for fleeting moments of pleasure, however long they would last.

"Max... Q..."

I heard the familiar masculine voice in the room and realized it was my turn to be caught out. Max and I broke apart, panting as we tried to recover from our kiss. He lowered me to the floor, turning his head to find the last person on earth who needed to see us that way.

Oh fuck.

Chapter Fifteen

MAX

DAMMIT. All that shit I'd just spouted on and on about, doing the right thing, being the reliable one... all of it, was just proven to be bullshit as my brother caught me with my hands on his girl's ass. Quivina probably hadn't lied about telling him she wasn't interested romantically, but what I'd just done violated every bro-code in the book.

"Man, I can explain..." My first thought was to defend myself because that's what sorry fuckers like me did. And it usually started with *I can explain*.

"So... that's what all that shit was about earlier? You being pissed at me? Dog, this shit... this shit here is fucked-up." His voice was a whisper, nearly cracking from the pain of the knife in his back.

"Pronto, I should have told you I was thi—"

"You're damn right, Q. And don't call me that. You don't get to use something so personal. You should have told me, and so should he," he snapped.

"Aye, man, it's about me and you. Quivina tried to tell

you she was going through some things. This just happened. I swear it did." I looked at my brother and stepped away from Quivina. It couldn't have been helpful to the situation that we were practically attached at the hips.

"Nothing just happens, Max. You always have to come out on top, don't you? You swoop in and take care of the kids for Cami, looking like the big man. You take Q because you're the intellectual one." Smith's head swung back and forth like he was trying to shake puzzle pieces into place. "Even in a crash that should have killed us, you walk away without a scratch. And I walk away... oh shit, that's right. I couldn't fucking walk away."

"Smith..."

"Fuck you, Max. You win again, man. Congratulations, you sorry bastard." Smith turned around, and it was then that I remembered the kids in all our mess. Donnie looked back and forth between Smith and me like he didn't know whose side to take. Diane was looking down at the floor.

"I'm sorry, Smith..." Quivina called out.

"Yeah... you always are, Q." Smith kept walking and vanished out the door.

"So... are we staying here for the night?" Donnie asked.

I'd totally forgotten that Smith mentioned coming over to get his tie. I assumed he had done it earlier in the day, after he'd gotten the kids. I guess I was wrong. "Yeah. Do me a favor and go to your rooms so I can talk to Ms. Quivina, okay? We'll figure out dinner later."

They both nodded, and Diane gave a wave to Quivina as they walked past to their bedrooms. "It was nice to meet you," she said, always polite to her elders, even when the circumstances weren't the best.

Quivina gave a wave and weak smile. Once they were gone, she turned her attention to me. "I'm going to go...

yeah, I should leave." She sounded like she was debating staying.

The truth was, I needed her to go. The things Smith had said to me, the way I'd made him feel when he was one of the most important people in the world to me, was like coarse sandpaper to my skin, rubbing me raw. My heart ached because it had been the absolute last thing I wanted to do.

"I think that's best," I said.

Moments before, Quivina had been all I could see. She was the only woman to ever make me forget about the vows I'd taken for my family. But maybe I didn't need to forget anymore. Even if it was the best feeling I'd had in a very long time.

"Okay..." she said, sucking in a breath and already moving to gather her things. "I shouldn't have put you in that position. It was wrong."

It was there I had to stop her. "Quivina, you weren't wrong to want to kiss me and I wasn't to take the chance. I don't regret that... not that moment with you. I do feel bad about my brother. He doesn't deserve th... what he just saw."

"I don't regret it, either. I just wish I'd been clearer with him. I honestly don't want you to harm your relationship with him. I gather things haven't been good since the accident and I don't know exactly what happened. Maybe I wouldn't have behaved so selfishly."

"There are a million maybes, but truthfully, there would have never been a good situation for us as long as you dated my brother. It was always going to be bad. But we can't go back. Only forward. You can't ever correct history." I didn't add anything else. I wanted to tell her how much I liked her, but it wasn't the right time. As silence fell around us, I watched her consider what I'd said.

"You're right, Max. I can't unhurt Smith. But that doesn't make me want you any less. I know you have a lot to sort through with your family, and I need to reach out to Smith so he knows how I feel." Her eyes were filled with emotion as she looked at me before giving me a twisted smile.

Before she could get away, I grabbed her by both hands and pulled her gently into a soft kiss. "I know this feels all wrong right now, but whatever is meant to be, will be. Once things settle a bit, we can go on an official date."

"I think I'd like that. Hopefully, we can put both our relationships with Smith back right."

"I hope so. As much as I love my brother, I don't know how I can let you go." It was probably too much, given the circumstances, but it was my truth. Quivina made me feel like I could start over again.

"I know... I feel the same way. I really should get out of here, though. The kids are probably confused and need you to sort things out for them." She squeezed my hands, since I was still holding on to hers, and I released them. When she turned to walk to the front door, I followed behind her.

I reached around her to open the door, something that was becoming a habit as she left my apartment. I made it a point to brush against her, needing to feel her soft skin against mine once more. There was no way to know when I'd see her again.

"Good night, Max."

"'Night, Quivina." I leaned against the doorframe and watched as she headed for the stairs.

With her departure, all the bad memories started to flood into my mind. My brother didn't deserve what I'd just put him through. I was so greedy to have her that I'd forgotten about Smith. Forgotten I'd already had his trust and lost it the day of the accident. Every day he'd been in my life since then had been a gift. And I'd forsaken it all for her mouth, her hands, her body against mine.

The converse emotion, the one hiding in the darkness, was the joy of having kissed her. If I'd been someone else, some other guy who hadn't cost his brother his career, I would have been still wrapped up in her and loving every minute of it.

I stepped back into my apartment and looked for something to eat. I gave up halfway through and decided on takeout. "Kiddos," I called to my niece and nephew. Walking over to my couch, I slumped into it and scrubbed a hand over my face, waiting for them to appear.

"Yes, Uncle Max," Donnie said as he entered the living room.

Diane was not far behind him.

"I'm getting takeout. What would you two like?"

"Um... I think I want a sandwich from that place we went to... I don't remember the name, but it was good," he said.

"No, I want some tacos from—"

"Ugh, YouTube says it's not real meat," Donnie shot back to Diane.

"YouTube isn't the boss of me. I want some tacos."

"We always have to do what you want, Diane." He sang her name in the universal tone of annoyance.

"I'll get both. Okay? That way everybody is happy," I said.

They both turned to look at me, partly because I never agreed to fast food. I was just as against it as Donnie was. Diane was elated, Donnie confused.

"Okay... do you want to play a video game with me when you're done, Uncle Max?"

Donnie never asked me to do anything with him, so the question left me puzzled. I looked over at the kid, his hair a little too long on the sides. I would have to take him for a haircut soon. He reminded me of Odell Beckham, without the blond. "Yeah," I replied. "Let me order GrubHub and then we can play your video game while we wait."

"Cool, I'll bring it out here." He disappeared into the back, and Diane came and sat on the couch near me.

"Are you and Uncle Pronto mad at each other?" Diane leaned over and curled against me.

My family was a unit. We'd always been in each other's lives, in one another's affairs, barging in and taking over. Or at least, I barged in and took over. After my father died, I'd promised to take care of them, despite my stepmother telling me I was still just a kid. I had been angry with my father because of his drinking, yet I'd been the one to tear us all apart. "No... well, yeah. I did something—"

"You kissed his girlfriend," she said pointedly.

"I did not, exactly. They were friends, and Ms. Quivina and I are friends. It's complicated."

"At school, Geneva Brown told Avery Massey that she would fight her if she didn't leave her boyfriend alone."

"Aren't you guys too young for boyfriends?"

"Well, I don't have a boyfriend. I don't think I want one either, especially if it makes you want to fight someone."

"It shouldn't... but I guess, yeah... Smith and I are in a similar situation to Geneva and Avery."

"But which one are you?"

"I guess I'd be Avery." My familiar friend, guilt, crept into my chest with its heavy paws and sat there. "But your uncle and I aren't going to fight."

Donnie came back into the room and began plugging his system into my flatscreen TV. "I think Uncle Pronto is probably really good at fighting," he said.

"We aren't going to fight." I sat up and opened my app to order our dinner.

"Good. Because I think he might win, Uncle Max. He works out all the time."

"I know," I said.

"He eats all organic food," he said.

I rolled my eyes. "I know."

"And he does MMA training. Please don't fight him, Uncle Max."

"What sandwich do you want? The wrap with the cranberries?" I asked.

"Yes. Did you hear me? I don't want you to get beat up."

I had actually almost had it. "What makes you think I can't fight?" My ego got the better of me, and I nearly finger-punched my cell phone into oblivion.

"Well... you run a lot, but that doesn't build muscle. That's what Uncle Pronto told me. He builds muscle. *Super Mario Kart.*" He expanded his hands as the game intro flashed onto the screen and brought the controllers over to me.

"Hang on one sec. I need to finish our order."

"Okay. But if you're going to fight Uncle Pronto, try to postpone it so you can build up some muscle. It shouldn't take too long," he advised.

"Got that," I said.

"Donnie, stop telling Uncle Max he's skinny," Diane added.

"He didn't say I was skinny." Not sure what exactly I was defending in that statement.

"He did. He said you didn't have muscle. That means you're..."

"No, I'm pretty sure that's not what that meant," I said.

"Donnie, do you think Uncle Max is skinny?"

"Not real, real skinny, but he's for sure not built like Uncle Pronto."

"Is this body-shaming? Are you two body-shaming

me?" I finished up the order and laid the phone on the couch, realizing of course that my brother got all the athleticism, and I got all the... well, Smith was smart too, so I couldn't even claim all the brains. Shit... Quivina had to be confused. Surely, she wanted Smith over me.

"I'm not body-shaming you. I just don't think you should fight Uncle Pronto. Besides his training, you are brothers. And y'all always tell me and Diane not to fight. We're all we have in the end. Right?" Donnie handed me the controller and gave me a direct stare. The condescending glare kids got when they knew the adults were fucking shit up. Although, I don't think I was ever as smart as those two at their age.

"You're absolutely correct. Siblings shouldn't fight. I'm going to apologize to your uncle for—"

"Kissing his girlfriend like Avery Massey," Diane added.

"Yes. That's exactly what I'll do," I said.

Chapter Sixteen

I HAD A KISS HANGOVER. Never in my life had I been so gone, so categorically in lust with a man over a kiss. I'd thought about it all night, dreamt of him—his hands on my body as I inhaled his scent, his tongue exploring my mouth with such hunger and need, the feeling of his body between my thighs as I wrapped myself around him. Our connection was scintillating, every moment scored into my memory.

I had gone to my car after leaving his place and fallen asleep for a while, giving my brain permission to freely conjure his beautiful face in my mind. It would have been wonderful except each time ending with Pronto... Smith. I was to call him Smith, he'd said. His face, normally smiling and kind, had turned into a mask of confusion, then pain. I'd done that. We had been on dates, but in the end, I told him my truth. That I wasn't ready. What I should have said was I wasn't ready for him. He hadn't deserved it. But Smith was such a wonderful person, he would find someone. And once he stopped to think about it, he would know I was right. Ours was the stuff of friendships, not lovers.

I didn't even have Nell to talk things over with. When I got back to the apartment later in the evening, her door was closed. In the morning, it was still closed. I assumed her friend had stayed over, and considering how much I'd seen of our guest, I didn't want to add to the embarrassment. So, I got a bowl of oatmeal and left the house without talking over my problem with my very best friend.

Instead, I pondered the circumstances I'd found myself in and deduced it was pretty much hopeless. The fact remained that despite our kiss and shared intimacy, Max was still distant. I wanted to break down his wall, but I wasn't sure I could. Not with the problem I'd caused by dating his brother. It was an unfair truth, but truth, nonetheless. I wished I could go back to the first day we'd met and redo it somehow. Knowing what I knew of probability, there was practically no chance we'd be able to course correct and get back on the right track. Even if you left in infinity, there would be no way to round up to happiness.

I made it to school the next day, and despite having no disruptions since there were no 360Project classes on Friday, I was still busy. The first week had been exhilarating, at least from a work perspective. I enjoyed being back in front of the students again. It was like going home.

I sat at my desk in the shared office space for adjunct faculty members and looked over some of the grades. We'd taken a placement test to see what level the students were in math, and most had been in need of some tutoring. I didn't know what campus resources would be available for them after the term was over, but I made a mental note to ask Max what I could do to help in that capacity.

It would have been a lot easier if he weren't my advisor too. As I opened the email to send off a note to him, I wondered if he would think I was making something up to communicate with him. Shit... while it was work-related, I wasn't sure whether he would want to hear from me just yet.

I must have started it fifteen or twenty times, hitting compose, typing *hello*, or *hi*, then just his name, then *hey*. After each time, I closed the email and had to go through the trouble of hitting compose once more.

Ridiculous. I was being obsessive over an email. More than excessive, I was being paranoid about the way he would receive it. If I'd never kissed him, I would have just marched into his office. Hell, I didn't even have his cell phone outright. It had been included in the introductory info about 360Project, but it wasn't mine to exploit for my own gain.

How sad was I that I couldn't even muster up the courage to go ask a damn question?

I ran a hand over my short hair and liked the way it bristled against my fingers. The sigh that followed wasn't one of relief, however. I needed to focus on other things... it was obvious I was becoming a bit burdensome to Nell given she couldn't even have a sex life, the situation with my father was more than enough to deal with on its own, and I was on the verge of becoming a whole new independent person— something I had never been. Man trouble should take a backseat to all that drama.

I knew Nell had been right when she finally agreed to what I'd been saying all along. I didn't need a boyfriend. I needed to figure all my mess out. And that messy situation with Max and his brother was like a confirmation of what I should have started all along. First, I'd find a place to live, then I would work out all the things that were at the root of why I'd married a man I didn't completely love in the first place. I kind of knew when that started. It was when I was a little girl and every woman I'd ever known told me how important it was to find a husband, every princess movie I'd ever watched, and somehow, the message that girls were nothing unless a boy wanted them took hold of my psyche. From then on, I wrapped myself into a little box and deemed men more important than myself.

If I were ever going to be ready for another relationship, I would have to deconstruct the mental matter playing that same song over and over in my mind. Yes, I was attracted to Max, but love was not a part of it. Even if it was, I needed to be okay with myself before I could have any sort of success in that department.

So, I wouldn't send the email. I shut down my Outlook and focused on ensuring that the grades were added to the system, a mandate of the program to identify any downward trends before they became problematic. I hunkered down and did my job. The one I'd wanted so badly and had been thrilled to get was right in front of me, and I was missing out on how wonderful it was to live out one of my accomplishments. With my goal at the forefront instead of someone else for a change, I was able to concentrate. Over an hour later, I was surprised to hear the knock on the door to the adjunct offices. No one ever knocked, since they weren't private offices.

"Come in," I responded.

The door opened slightly, and before I saw anyone, I heard, "It's me... um, Max Wynn..." He popped his head around the door and gave a tight smile.

I could see him clearly due to the lack of walls in our lounge. He looked tired and concerned, so much so, he'd said his last name as if we were strangers.

"Yes, Max," I said, more like a parrot than an actual response. I could see in his face what he was there to tell me. I knew with all my soul that he was backing away from the one-and-a-half intimate moments we'd shared. "Come over and have a seat."

He walked inside the room, hands shoved down in the pockets of his slim-cut black trousers. His was absent his signature jacket, present even on the hottest days, but wore a denim button-down that made him look like he had the day I'd met him, casual yet in a runway-model kind of way. Maybe that had more to do with his confident stride, lean build, and height than his actual outfits.

"How are you?" Max made it to the chair and turned to look around the room before taking a seat. Another red flag.

"I'm good, considering I spent half the night asleep in my car." The old Quivina would have never acknowledged her own discomfort. But I was tired of her. I wanted to be the new me, who said what was on her mind. No time like the present to start.

"Oh, I'm sorry. If I'd known you were going to—"

"No, no. You needed to tend to the kids. I knew that. Family infrastructures are very fragile when dealing with illness. You need to make sure to patch every fissure. You know what I mean?" I spoke from my own experience with my father when my mother had passed away. Our relationship had never been the same after that, deteriorating until there was nearly nothing left and unable to withstand even the slightest change.

"I do... it's... it's tenuous, at best. Thank you for understanding," he said.

"No problem. Now, what did you come to see me about? It can't be sleeping in my car."

Max let out an uncomfortable chuckle. "No, not that." He took in a breath and started again. "I wanted to talk about us and... the way we left things. I don't think we can —" He made a gesture between us, letting me know I was right about my presumption. He was there to call it off.

"Max," I said, placing my hands on either of his, "I know we can't date one another." My voice was, surprisingly, monotone, none of the actual chaos inside me breaking through. I wasn't even sure if what I was about to say was the right thing to do. But I was done overthinking things. I wanted to feel something.

"I was going to say we probably needed to hold off... just until I figure things out with Smith." There was pleading in his eyes.

"I know... I know what you're trying to do. You want to smooth things over with your brother, and I get that. Family relationships are very important."

Max reclined in the chair and ran a hand over the back of his neck. "That obvious, huh?"

"Let's just say it doesn't take a PhD in physics to figure it out... yet I have one, so it took me all of a couple of seconds to understand your backstory. The accident that took Smith's leg? You were the driver... which makes it really important for you to show your entire family you love them. Sound about right?"

From Max's wince and repositioning in his seat, I knew I'd found the x in the equation. "Well... maybe not overcompensating, but—"

"Your word, not mine. But you know what, I don't want to be in the middle of something so hard. I have my own crazy family dynamic. My father would never get past me divorcing a surgeon to be with a professor. What's worse than that? An American professor... or—"

"Someone like me?"

"Well, my father is old-school," I said, skirting the blatant statement. Maybe I wasn't all the way into the new me just yet. "He would like for me to be with my ex-husband."

"Despite what you believe?"

"Oh yeah. My parents believed you work through problems, not run from them. In his eyes, I am a coward. But that's another story. We're dealing with the situation we've found ourselves in. It's unavoidable."

"What is?"

"That fact that even after a hiatus of sorts, we probably won't be able to be together. Especially if you and Pron... Smith can't get past your differences. They're pretty deeply rooted. But I have a proposition."

Max leaned forward a bit, studying me. His eyes roved over my face and then narrowed as if he was suspicious of what I would say next.

Shit, so was I. But I continued, nerves balling in the pit of my stomach and tightening until I could barely breathe. "I think we should spend this weekend together, probably at a hotel so we aren't disturbed, and explore what won't ever be..." The last bit kind of slurred out, as if the knot in my stomach were trying to keep me from saying the words.

"You mean... working out this... tension between us?"

"I do. I think it would be good for us to see what it's about and then we can retreat to our corners to deal with all our issues. I have a lot and so do you. But, I resolved dating may be off the table for me until I figure out a few things about myself. I want you, though. And while I know we have to be responsible, I haven't ever had anything that was just for me. This is it. My one thing. I know it sounds ridiculous, yet..."

My words ran out. I didn't know what else to say. Max looked wholly skeptical of my suggestion, and I frankly didn't blame him. It was as if I thought of him as an object. And I didn't, but I knew it would be a very, very long time before I got involved, for my own good. I was foolish to buy into the notion of us being together. And even Nell had agreed I needed to focus on myself. And his silence was going on too long, so maybe... "You know what, forget I said anything, Max. It was—"

"Okay."

"...stupid of me," I finished. "What?" Our words had bumped into one another, and I wasn't sure what I'd just heard.

"I said, okay. One weekend."

"Okay..." I replied. "But what will you tell Smith?"

"What you just said. We can't possibly be together. I had some personal shit to deal with and so do you. I'll just omit the part about us making love."

"Sleeping together. Or fucking. Not making love." It was crass, but I couldn't even start to think of what we had just agreed to as anything other than what it was. My mind wasn't ready for the seriousness of all that.

"Okay, then. We're going to fuck. This weekend, and whatever happens, we'll be able to walk away from one another." Max's eyes smoldered as he said the words.

I straightened in my seat, trying hard to smother the flames that ignited at my core. "Without even a glance back. We'll work together and be nothing more than colleagues going forward. Deal?"

"It's a deal. The kids are going to be with Smith until Sunday to make up for last night. My niece told me he'd texted her and asked her to let me know."

"You still haven't spoken to him, huh?"

"No, he won't accept my calls. But I don't want to talk about him right now. I thought about the guy all night with the exception of... well, when I was thinking about you, since we're laying our cards on the table."

"Well, at least now we'll have the ability to do some of the things we thought about last night." My heart was hammering in my chest as I continued down my new path. I hadn't ever been a woman who spoke openly about what I wanted, but even as I was about to collapse into a bundle of nerves, excitement quivered in my marrow.

Max leaned forward, his elbows pressed into the desk as he rose slightly and moved directly into my face. His salted ocean scent enveloped me. "I'm going to have to hold you to that."

My lips puckered ever so slightly of their own volition. I cleared my throat and made an effort to not look so damned thirsty. "You should," I whispered.

The sound of footsteps in the hallway seemed to press Max down into his chair and farther away from me. The promise of his kiss snatched away at the last moment left a burning sensation over my lips. I turned to look at who was entering. Candace, the annoying girl who always wanted to touch my hair or see if we could wear the same pink lipstick, breezed into the room. "Hi, Professor Wynn. I'm so excited about the Inspiration Alley you came up with," she said, sultry and enthusiastic at the same time.

"Actually, that was Professor Adedeji's idea." He unfolded himself from the chair and pulled his shirt down tightly over his pants. I imagined it was to cover a raging erection, just as I was holding my arm awkwardly over my breasts to cover ice-hard nipples.

"If you two will excuse me, I need to get back." Max gave a nod in both our directions and left the room in what seemed to be an effort to make himself look unhurried.

At least I knew then, from his board-stiff walk and the feeling as if his hands were all over me even after he left, my message was well received.

"Well," Candace piped, her voice noticeably different than moments earlier, "I guess congratulations are in order."

"I guess so," I replied, trying like hell and unequivocally failing at hiding my smile.

Chapter Seventeen

MAX

WHAT HAD I gotten myself into? I wouldn't have been able to say no even if I'd tried. But at the rate I was going, I was going to blow before I even got to her. I booked a room at the Westin and texted Smith to see if he was going to for sure keep the kids for the entire weekend—to which I'd received a one-word answer of *yup*. Despite the severity of all we'd been through in the past, this time seemed more finite. And I wasn't quite sure what to do with that.

I stopped by the hospital to tell Cami about where the kids would be and she saw right through my shit.

"What's going on with you and Pronto?" Her eyes were narrower than normal, and she'd crossed her arms over her chest.

"Nothing. He just had to leave the other night so he couldn't keep them. He didn't want to disappoint them."

"So, why aren't you two speaking?" More slitted-eye glare.

"We're talking..." More like he yelled at me that I was an

asshole and wouldn't return my calls, but those were technicalities.

"Well, why did he call me to tell you he would drop the kids off at camp on Monday and not to worry about the bags?"

"Girl, you are on one today. I was in meetings all day. I told you about the 360Project events we're having... it's time-consuming, that's all. Stop worrying." The lie burned at my chest. It wasn't something I would have normally done, but in order to spare my already drained sister a moment of concern about me and Smith, I swallowed the truth. I walked over to her hospital bed and leaned down to kiss her forehead.

Cami wrapped her frail arms around me, and I realized how weak, how small she was in comparison to when she'd first gotten sick. She was doing better with keeping food down, but the weight would take some time. My heart clenched at the thought, but I tried pushing it away. She didn't need me to break on her.

"All right. Don't fight. We're all we have," she whispered into my shoulder.

"I know. You don't worry about us." I pulled back after giving her one more squeeze. "We're gonna be okay. All of us."

"I'm holding you to that shit. Now, I can see you fidgeting. Get going to wherever the heck you're hurrying off to. I love you, brother."

"I love you too, sis. I'll see you soon."

I gave her one more glance back before leaving, and she had already rolled onto her side and picked up her remote. Her roses from earlier that week were wilting, and I made a mental note to bring her more. I left the room without crying or being on the verge of a breakdown for the first time in... well, damn near ever. And it was because of Quivina. She'd helped me begin to hope again.

I resolved for a change to let it all go as I waited for the elevator to take me to the lobby level. My problems with Smith, my sister's health... all of it. Because for the weekend, I would be with Quivina. When was the last time I'd been excited about anything? I didn't know, but the feeling in my chest was as foreign as the sensation in my cock.

I replayed her words again and again throughout the day... *Fucking. Not making love...* I'd damn near come in my pants as she said it. Her red lipstick laboring over the syllables was the image burned into my mind. I wanted to ruin the color, smearing it all over her mouth with my own. It had been an eternity since I'd been with anyone I actually wanted. She was like the deep inhale after emerging from underwater, or the cool rain on an overly humid day. She was everything in a beautiful package, one I couldn't wait until Christmas Day to open.

Well, that weekend would be Christmas. Over and over again.

How was it someone I'd spent the sum total of maybe two days with was consuming me? Back when my father had been alive, he'd told me when he met his second wife, he just knew he had to have her. It was a foreign concept for me since I'd never needed to pursue any woman. In fact, what was happening with Quivina was something altogether new. Before her, I would have easily just let her go with Smith. I wouldn't have kissed her. And I for damn sure wouldn't be sneaking off to a hotel to spend a weekend with her... it was ridiculous. As horrible as it sounded, I never even cried or spent an uncomfortable moment when getting my divorce. It was just another chapter coming to an end. Another part of history, annotated as a lesson learned and to be moved on from.

But even when she asked and I knew it was just about the craziest notion I'd ever heard, I couldn't stop myself from saying yes. Because I wanted her too. I wanted her so badly, I'd considered whacking my wayward cock on the faculty bathroom sink to make the damn thing soft. I could hardly even sit down. Fortunately, after several minutes thinking about the Bible and the way oatmeal looked when it was being stirred, I was able to freely sit and stand, even if still semi-erect.

I practically broke every driving rule on the way there. I wanted to beat her to the room and watch her eyes as she walked into the suite with the roses and champagne I'd ordered. If we were going to do it one weekend, then I wanted her to remember it forever.

I made it first, and damn... I nearly didn't believe it myself. I hadn't ever been one to pop for the big suite, mostly because when I was on vacation, I didn't spend much time in the room. And I was a professor, after all. But something about Quivina made me want to splurge on her. She deserved it. And as she'd talked to me earlier, I could see she was being sincere. She was giving me what I needed, even if I hadn't verbalized it and despite how she truly felt. There weren't many people in the world who were so selfless.

I appreciated her for doing it. I had never had such a positive experience with a woman when deciding not to see one another again. At the moment though, I was pacing around the opulent room like a lunatic. I didn't spring for the rose petals on the bed nor any other cheesy thing in the hotel amenities. It wasn't that type of night. We were trying to do this one time—get in and get out, so to speak. It was unlikely that I would easily forget about Quivina, yet I would do anything for her.

As I thought of it, a slight ache formed in my chest. I ran my knuckles up and down over the spot along my ribcage.

In another minute, I heard the ding of the elevator. There were only two other suites on the floor, so I knew she was coming. I glanced down at myself. I hadn't changed from my trousers and shirt. I still looked polished, and for that I was thankful. I heard her key card beep to let her in. In an effort to appear cool and collected, I leaned against the dresser and watched as she stepped inside. Honestly, I was anything but collected as my heart rammed against my ribcage. Quivina made me feel things I never had before, and as wonderful as it was, I was terrified... and elated by the very sight of her. The warm glow of the lamps on both sides of the room lit her path as she stepped to the center of the floor.

"Hi," she said. "Have you been here long?" She moved closer to me and gave a sly smile.

"I just got here," I lied. I was surprised there wasn't tread on the carpet from the twenty minutes I'd spent circling like a shark with the fresh scent of blood in the water.

"Oh, good. I was anxious... maybe that's not the best word. I was excited to see you."

"I couldn't wait for you to get here either." I slid my hands into my pockets and found their bottoms with my fingertips.

"Well, let's not spend all our time talking..."

I watched as she pulled the long top that resembled a shirt over her head and laid it on the bed.

I couldn't do anything but savor the view of her ebony skin. Quivina was sexy as hell. I could almost taste her, the memory of her sweet mouth on mine heightening my antici-pation. My cock immediately discarded all thoughts of oatmeal and Proverbs, the shreds of my momentary distrac-tions long gone with one look at her smoky gray high-heeled sandals like studded cages around her feet, black lace panties, and matching bra.

"Quivina, I'm not trying to be a buzzkill," I started, warring with myself over my next words. I didn't want to say it, but I had to, for both our sakes, "but, our relationship can't be more than this. I can't risk my fam—"

"Max, this is one time. I'm not exactly ready for a relationship either. If you're having second thoughts, though, we don't have to do this." Quivina crossed her arms over her chest, clutching her elbows in an attempt to cover herself.

"No... no, I want you so badly. I only wanted to give you a chance to back out if... in case you want more from someone."

"This is probably the worst time to be having this conversation."

My dick twitched like it agreed with her. Goddamn traitor. I crossed the room in just a few strides and captured her chin just as she began to lower her head in what resembled defeat. "I know it's the worst timing in the world, but Quivina...." I stared at her until her gaze returned to my face. "I won't be able to stop myself once we start. And if you were to have second thoughts after I'm so close to the only thing I've been able to think about since we kissed, I'd probably never be right again." I released her chin, then ran my hands over her shoulders.

"I don't think I can turn back now... I-I'm pretty sure I'm obsessed with you. As pathetic as that sounds, I need this moment. And while it's fleeting, if we don't take this further, it will be one of my life's greatest regrets."

Something twisted inside me, my gut or my heart or some other vital organ turning itself inside out as warmth spread over my body. "It's not pathetic. It's mutual," was all I could manage before I claimed her mouth. I pressed my tongue against her lips, demanding entry inside her. I had this hunger for her that had only managed to intensify the more I tried to convince myself I couldn't have her. And as evil as it sounded, I was glad Smith wouldn't have her either. I wouldn't be able to stand watching them grow old together.

The more I thought of him and her, the more desperate I became, our kiss deepening, her hands on my waist, mine on her naked skin, the feeling of silk beneath my fingertips.

I needed her.

Quivina ran her hands up my sides, over my shoulders, and finally around my neck. Her body strained against mine we tried to navigate my height to her stature. I bent down more to keep our connection, my tongue ever exploring her inside, her minty taste filling me, the grip of lust fusing us together.

"I need to feel you inside me," she breathed into my mouth.

Oh no, I thought. "You aren't getting off that easy." I lifted her, my hands behind her thighs urging her to wrap her legs around me. We kept on kissing, my greedy mouth devouring hers, her mouth open and panting around mine. I bit at her plump lower lip while walking her across the suite and stumbling into the bedroom. Fortunately, I remembered where the bed was.

The lazy summer sun was dropping from the sky, but I could see all of her as I laid her on the bed.

She let out a sigh as her body fell away from mine in the shift from standing to lying down. I moaned as I slid down her body, kissing my way over her stomach, over the silken cover of her mound. "Do you like these panties at all?" I looked up at her face to find her staring from under lowered lids.

"Not enough to care what happens to them. Not right now..." Her voice was huskier than I'd ever heard it, almost as if she were holding back a growl.

"Good." Taking the crotch with my index finger, I

wrapped the soaked seat around it and twisted them to the side. My knuckle stroked against her plump sex, her essence spilling warm on my skin. I lowered my mouth to her slit and glanced up to her once more. She was gripping the floral bedspread tight in her hands.

I licked my lips in an effort to show her how hungry I was. To taste her. To indulge in her. I lowered my head to her and leisurely licked along her slit. Parting the soft hairs with my tongue, I tasted her sweetness. When I reached the top, I locked my arms around her thighs to keep her in place and pressed inside, my thumbs spreading her open so I could fully access her tight nub.

Her thighs trembled, and soft moans rose and fell as I massaged her most intimate place. I opened my mouth wide to suck nearly the whole of her sex, and she cried out, my name strung alongside *Jesus* and *oh*s in a crescendo. I released the pressure and blew against her sex, careful not to give her a quick release. I wanted her to remember every part, to make it long and passionate.

After another lingering lick of the center, I closed in on her clit, alternating between sucking and blowing and kissing, moving seamlessly between low and high intensity. I could feel her coming undone around me, and I loved every second of it.

Repositioning, I slipped two fingers inside her while suckling her and pressed inside, at first slow and careful, then faster, feeling the soft ribbons of flesh as her internal muscles tightened around my fingers. She pumped against my mouth, her back arching from the bed. "Oh God, oh my God," she purred.

"Tell me how it feels," I replied, turning my head enough for her to hear my demand. My dick was rod straight, and I pressed my hips inward, the hard bedframe and comforter providing enough resistance to keep me from coming.

"Oh, Max... it's so good." Her squeaky pitch told me I was hitting the right spot.

I dove in again, my tongue relentlessly seeking every nerve ending beneath her sensitive flesh, my fingers driving deeper and deeper inside her body.

"Yes, Max, yes..."

I tripled the speed of my fingers and tongue, ready to give her the release she was desperately trying to pump out. Her thighs were the first indication, tightening around my neck. Quivina lifted her ass, serving her glorious pussy up for me to continue my ministrations on her sex. I didn't let up, eager to hear her voice reach yet another octave.

"I can't... I'm coming... shit, I'm coming."

Her hips rocked hard against me, and I held her thigh tight with my free hand, the other buried inside her as bands of muscle clenched and released in a fever pitch.

Quivina came and came and came against me, using my mouth to wring out every ounce of pleasure she could get.

I pulled away once her bucking stopped and watched as she pulled her legs up and wrapped her arms around her knees. She rocked back and forth in the fetal position as if she was trying to hold the sensation inside her.

I crawled onto the bed and wrapped my arms around her, then pulled her body against mine. "That good huh?"

"Oh Max, I can't even begin..." She allowed the rest of her sentence to trail off. "But we still have more, right?" Quivina shifted around in my arms and kissed me, softly, then stared with lowered lids.

"Oh baby, you have no idea." We were only just getting started.

Chapter Eighteen

THE HEAT of his kiss and touch were still warm on my skin. I could barely breathe so close to him, yet I inhaled to take in his scent that reminded me of the sea. I could see his eyes trained on me by the dim glow of the bathroom's light. The sun set completely while Max had me otherwise occupied, and neither of us moved to remedy the situation. We were caught up in one another, and while I wanted him inside me, I was enjoying the few moments of just lying close to him. I couldn't make out his expression in the darkened room, but I hoped he looked as goofy as I thought I did.

I watched as he grasped my hand in his and kissed my knuckles, the heat of his mouth reminding me of the rub of his whiskers between my thighs. I couldn't make out all of his features in the darkness, but my mind filled in a sly smile as mischief played in his eyes. "Don't go anywhere. I'm going to get a condom and make good on my promise."

A shot of cold nerves ran the length of my spine, and I

stiffened, thankful Max wasn't still on the bed. I was all bravery and sex goddess when I'd propositioned him earlier but now, lying there waiting for him to get a condom, I remembered all the things that had kept me from dating in the first place. I'd never been with another man besides Kenyon. And while I'd never felt anything close to what Max made me feel with my ex, a part of me was distracted by all the things my ex had put me through.

Kenyon told me I was terrible in bed and that I was the worst lay he'd ever had. The stage fright gripped me so hard, I had to pull my knees into my chest, wrapping them with my arms.

"I'm not going anywhere," I said to myself. I pushed the negative thoughts from my mind and watched as Max turned on the light and illuminated the suite. He seemed to have spared no expense. In my nervousness, I'd missed all the opulence, and the fact that he looked damned sexy. He stood before me wearing a white button-down shirt open to reveal his abs and the women-stupefying V-cut leading into his trousers. I knew there were so many other things to worry over, but one look at him and the thoughts fled.

"This isn't an ideal situation, Quivina, I know. But right now, I can't think of anywhere else I want to be." Max pulled a condom from his pants, then as if he'd willed them off, they slid down his body. He slowly rolled down his boxers to reveal his erection, standing at attention and glossed on the tip as if in anticipation.

His words should have made perfect sense to me, but not while I was watching him run the pre-cum down his shaft, followed by the sleeve he stretched wide to accommo-date his girth. My mouth went dry, and warmth flooded my pussy. I wanted him with an intensity I hadn't felt in what seemed like ages.

"Uh-huh," I replied to his forgotten statement.

He only smirked at me before stripping his shirt free from his body. "Girl, you're gonna drive me insane with the way you look."

I really wasn't that girl. I would have never been someone to walk into a room and strip, but I'd wanted to. I'd nearly lost the nerve and then I'd thought, what would Nell do? She would seize her moment with someone she wanted, that's what. It was the single motivation to even ask Max, and then to actually show up. "I guess I could say the same," I said.

This time, he didn't smirk. Instead, he walked over and kneeled beside me on the floor. "As much you can see that I want you, I can't do this if you aren't into it... into me. So much is going on around us, I wouldn't want to put you in a—"

"I asked you here, Max. I'm okay. And you're right, there is a lot going on for both of us. But doesn't that give us even more of a need for release? I'm not asking you to be my boyfriend. I'm asking you to make me feel good, for a small amount of time. We'll have to sort out your brother, my father, and what they mean to us later. Right now, I only want to do this." I leaned forward and brushed my lips against his in a slow kiss.

The growl coming from Max's chest let me know whatever concerns he had were gone, dissolved into a sea of desire.

His hands were on my hips in an instant, the power in them as he lay me back on the bed forcing my breath to come out in a rush. He closed his mouth over mine and kissed then stroked his tongue inside. My core erupted with heat, and I immediately wrapped my legs around his body, linking myself to him. His hardness against my near painfully tight clit as we rubbed savagely against one another. Everything was in that moment—every desire, every passing thought of us together, all the need and wanting that had built somehow into unbridled passion .

He hadn't even entered me, and I was on the verge of release, again.

We explored one another, his hands on my breasts, my mouth seeking his, our collective breathing scattered and wild.

I ran my hands over his sculpted back, feeling all the parts I had yet to see. When I reached his neck, I broke our kiss for one thing and one thing only. "Have me, Max." My voice was hoarse as if I'd been screaming, but the words escaped on nothing but a ragged whisper.

Max kissed down my neck and took one of my breasts into his mouth, rolling the nipple between teeth and tongue. I spasmed, my back raising from the bed, greedily seeking more, more, harder, and even harder still. I pulled at his neck, pressing him to my aroused nipple.

Max gingerly bit down, grazing his teeth over the sensitive flesh.

I could feel his hand traveling down, down his body to our centers, his hips rising slightly and his fingertips running the length of my wet slit. I moaned, my voice guttural and needy.

I felt him enter me, my body stretching to accommodate the width of his cock. I let my knees fall open onto the bed to give him all the room he needed, all I could afford him.

"Oh, damn." He slipped inside my body and sank in slowly until he could go no farther.

I was so full, so open for him. My body seemed to meld to his, and as he moved in and out, then in and out until we caught our rhythm with one another.

"Oh, Max... Max," I whimpered. His name was the only word I could form, my brain caught up in the moment, the magical feel of him driving into me.

Max leaned down and kissed me again, shifting his hips and reversing his stroke. I cried out into his mouth. What was he doing to me? How had I never felt this before?

I wanted to give him everything I'd never felt free enough to give before. I raised a leg as if our bodies knew how to move together, and he seamlessly hooked it over his shoulder.

When I thought he could go no deeper, he was inside me to his hilt. Our bodies slapped against one another as he increased speed, and I felt the flutters of my orgasm threatening release.

"Let me get on top, Max," I panted out, barely able to get the sentence into the world.

Max nodded, his mouth on my neck, as he rolled me over.

I looked down into his eyes to find them hazy with desire. He watched as I sat up on him, straddling his body, his hands now on my hips. "Quivina, I... damn, girl," he said.

I bit my lip. It was the first time I'd ever had sex with the light on, the first time I'd willingly wanted to straddle anyone, and I wanted it with Max. I rode him, slowly at first to get my groove, then faster once I adjusted to the sensation of him inside me. I wanted to feel him, to have an orgasm with him. I leaned forward, an angle that allowed me to keep him deep inside and to find a gentle stroke of my clit against his pelvis, and rocked back and forth. Max moaned, his mouth forming an O as he watched our bodies meet again and again with each rise and fall of my hips.

I felt the rise, the tingle, the urge to come with a burning urgency. I was nearly overcome with pleasure as he seemed to harden, to swell inside me. I leaned forward, pressed my mouth to his, and licked inside. His arms went to my waist, and he pulled me close. Breaking free of our kiss, I cried out, my torso arching away as I came apart. His mouth was on my breast again, and with the touch of his lips to my nipple, all the walls crumbled, my dam breaking open.

Max released my nipple amid a series of groans. "Fuck, Quivina, fuck me." His voice was guttural and primal, which let me know he was as gone in the moment as I was.

He pumped upward into me with ferocity, my body both taking and giving the most glorious satisfaction. "Max... this is... this is yours." Damned if I knew whether I meant it or not. I only knew it was true for however long it would last.

Max shuddered, his body fused to mine, and we came, erupted, finishing together as one.

I fell onto him, my energy spent, unable to even propel myself onto the bed. He draped himself around me the moment our chests met. His hands rubbed the length of my back, and I trembled in his arms.

"You can't be cold," he said, a light laugh following.

"I'm not... well, I don't... I don't know what I am," I admitted.

We shifted, and in an instant, a comforter was thrown over my back. I snuggled into his neck as he repositioned me farther down his chest, then folded me into his body with my arms hooked under his.

"It's okay. I don't know what I am either." The warmth of his lips pressed against my forehead as if to punctuate the statement.

I had so much to say to him, but in our silence, a sense of peace and warmth fell over us. It was... unlike anything I'd done after.... Well, after sex. Usually, there was this rush, as if I couldn't wait to get the other person off me. But with Max, I never wanted to be away from him. I could have lain like that forever.

I'm not even sure when we fell asleep, unaware of how

many minutes or hours had passed before I opened my eyes again. In the same position.

I lifted my head, thinking perhaps he was uncomfortable, but I found him asleep. I wanted to kiss him or rouse him, but Max was sleeping as if he had not done it in a very long time. Instead, I took a deep breath in, taking in the scent I was beginning to crave, then climbed off him and padded to the bathroom, softly closing the door behind me. He only shifted slightly as I pulled away from him, but his hands reached for me before I left the bed.

I glanced at myself in the mirror, surveying myself. My heart clenched in my chest. I wasn't the same girl I used to be, older and skin not as tight or as vibrant as it once was, but I looked new. My new hair, my cheeks flushed with a hint of red. I was... better.

It was a ridiculous notion. To think yourself a new person after an orgasm, but there I was. Unable to quit smiling and wanting to go back to bed with Max not even moments after I'd left him.

Well, however long it would last, I didn't want to miss a minute of it. I took care to freshen up and hurried out of the bathroom.

I closed the door behind me and turned around to find Max sitting up in the bed. The comforter was pulled up to his waist and he was staring at me with a heated gaze. "I thought you'd left when I first woke up. I was glad to hear the water going in the bathroom." He flipped the cover back for me to get in. "What we just did... I can't let you get away that fast." The corners of his mouth curved as he took in my body once more. The lights were still on, and while normally I was a lights-off girl, I didn't want to be that old person. Not anymore.

I bounded over to him, oblivious to how ridiculous it was to leap at a man. I jumped onto the bed and snuggled against him. "I wouldn't have left without saying goodbye."

"Good, all I could think was 'rude,'" he said.

"Well, considering how we met, I could see how you'd think that." I slipped beneath the covers and lay beside him, placing a hand on his stomach.

"True dat." We giggled as the thought of our first meeting flashed in my mind. "I have a question, though. I know about your divorce..."

"Umm-hmm." I ran my fingers over the thin trail of hair that ran down his stomach and disappeared beneath the covers.

"Well, you alluded to your father. I don't think I knew you were having family problems too." His eyes were sincere, brows furrowed as he studied my face.

I sat up and pulled the covers all the way up to cover my breasts. "It's nothing... just some stuff that's probably never going to be resolved." I tried to keep all the emotion out of my voice but knew I failed when Max tilted his head to the side and popped a brow.

"You know, I kind of have all the crazy on lock."

"Okay, you go first," I prodded.

"Room service first? Are you hungry? We worked up an appetite, and I'm not ready to leave this room yet."

The moment he said it, my stomach howled, a churning sound of hunger sounding out into the room. "Well, that answers that. I wasn't even thinking about food until you just said it."

"I should have taken you to dinner first. I'm sorry."

"Don't be silly. I probably would have insisted." I sat up and held a hand on my embarrassing stomach.

Max flipped the cover off and swung his legs off the bed. He grabbed a menu and handed it to me. "You choose. I'm pretty easy to please. And I've been eating vegetarian most nights since the kids started staying with me. It's too hard to cook multiple dinners."

"Hmm, okay. So, something for the carnivore in you?" I scanned the menu and found a surf-and-turf meal. "How about steak and lobster?"

"Well now, you know how to get me interested, don't you? I'll call it in. Anything to drink?"

"How about some wine?"

"Red, white, or pink?" he asked.

"Excuse me?" I tilted my head, trying to figure out what he was getting at.

"I was in NOLA and asked for a wine list. Let's just say it wasn't a five-star restaurant. Anyway, she said red, white, or pink. I was about to get into the various types in those three categories, but she stopped me. Said everything beyond that was inconsequential."

"And which did you end up taking?"

"Red."

"Was it good?"

"Not even a little bit, but at least the atmosphere was great."

For a moment, we nodded our agreement on all things awesome in New Orleans. "Yeah, atmosphere and who you're sharing space with can make even the worst things better..." This garnered a smile and for a moment, we simply stared at one another, drinking each other in.

He ordered our food, and I pulled on his shirt to cover myself. I hadn't even brought pjs. Most likely, my raging hormones had done a number on my practical side, just like they had banished my hunger momentarily.

I took a seat on the couch in the living room and waited for him. When he came out of the restroom, he wore his trousers. "Damn, you look way better than me in that shirt."

The smile came from my very soul, despite my internal

warning bells. He had a way with me. And I recognized that stone sober. After the wine arrived, I knew I was going to be a goner. "I'm so glad you weren't this guy in the parking lot the day I met you. I would have been in bed with you by the end of the day."

"Had I known that…"

"I'm serious. You are so charming when you want to be," I said.

He took the seat on the chair across from me. "Try telling that to my ex-wife."

"Yeah, only if you tell my ex-husband I'm cute."

"I never said you were cute. I said you look damn good. I said you were gorgeous."

"When did you say that?"

"I thought it the moment I saw you."

And it was that that stole my breath away.

Chapter Nineteen

MAX

"ALL RIGHT, quit stalling. Tell me about your father," I said.

Quivina was staring down at the remnants of steak and a half-eaten lobster tail. Her eyes popped back up to mine before they narrowed. "I thought it was you going first."

"Right... right." I set my plate back on the cart the server had left in the room for us. "So, we have had a hard time navigating our space since..." I ran a hand over my head, through my hair.

"Since the accident?"

"Yeah. I told you about the accident, but I didn't tell you what happened after... You see, my father died unexpectedly. He had a heart attack... it was one of those bad ones. You know," I said, my heart cracking open in my chest as I tried to get it out, "most people who have them have a five percent chance of survival."

"A widow-maker."

"Yeah. When we had the accident, he died. Like right

there… on the spot. It was remarkable…" My voice cracked as the last words left my mouth.

"Remarkable? It sounds tragic, Max. I'm so sorry."

"Yeah, well it was a long time ago. Thank you, though."

"You never talk about it, do you?"

"Not if I can help it. Most people don't want to hear about your troubles. They have enough of their own."

"Well, I'm asking. And we're still on the show-me-yours part."

Her smile gave me encouragement to continue. Something I hadn't had in a long time. "After my dad died, I was the one to help my stepmother with Smith, and Cami was younger, so… they never said it, but I knew… I knew they thought I destroyed their lives."

"Because of the accident?" she asked.

"Yeah. I was on my cell phone, arguing with my dad. He made me pick up Smith from football practice. I was… I was yelling at him and I came to a stop sign." I could still see the day so vividly even though it was over twenty years ago. "Even though I'd made the trip so many times, I forgot. I blew it going at least forty. When the first car hit, it was a T-bone on Smith's side. In between the crunch of metal and the blowing horns, it was almost as if I could hear Smith's bones, his life ripped away from him. As the car spun across the street, I saw the intermittent flashes of sun, the smoke from squealing tires released into the air, and the scent of gas as it spilled from the tank. In that space, I could almost believe we would be okay, even though my father was screaming for us to tell him what was going on from the phone. I could hear everything, my body like a tuning fork, torqued and white-knuckling the steering wheel. I thought we would be okay. Until the second hit, a truck slammed into us. The front of my car caved under the pressure and the entire front end was torn away. I didn't even know what happened until I woke up in the hospital."

Quivina was holding her mouth, all of what I'd told her written in horrifying detail over her face. "You both lived. That is…"

"I know. We had like a five percent chance of getting out of that crash alive. Both of us did, but Smith lost everything he'd worked so hard for"—I snapped my fingers together—"just like that."

We sat for a moment, neither of us speaking. I hadn't told anyone that story in as much detail.

"And you woke up to find your father had…" Her voice was almost a whisper. It let me know the entire thing was as bad as I thought.

"Guess the Wynn family had beaten enough odds for one day," I said.

Quivina stood from her spot on the sofa, my shirt hanging from her shoulders, her nakedness on full display. I should have been hard for her, but I wasn't. There was an unraveling inside my chest happening that stole every bit of my libido. She climbed onto my lap, straddling me, and pulled my head into her chest. "I'm so sorry, Max."

I couldn't do anything with the warmth wrapped around me except hug her. I threaded my arms around her waist and held on to her. For the first time since my father's funeral, tears flowed freely over my cheeks. "This isn't sexy at all," I said, laughing through my pain.

"It's okay. We can be unsexy together too."

Her hands stroked over the back of my head and down to my shoulders. I pulled her closer to me, allowing her sweet scent to fill my senses. "So, what about your family? Time for you to show me yours."

"Oh, my dad hates that I divorced my husband the

surgeon, despite his abuse and neglect. But let's save that one for breakfast, huh?"

We dissolved into one another, laughter mixed with more tears from both of us. I wasn't sure how it happened, but she kissed my forehead and something inside me awakened. I looked into her eyes, and our gaze held for seconds, minutes... I ran a fingertip down her face, feeling the warmth of her sex through my pants. I nudged her gently, pulling her into me.

I played with the hem of my shirt, holding on to it as if it were the only thing keeping me tethered to the planet, our anchor in a few hundred threads.

Quivina leaned forward, pressed her soft lips to mine, and kissed me. I wanted her so bad, the comfort within her arms, the feel of her softness against my ragged edges. She was a salve on my worn soul. I pulled away from her for a moment. I needed to tell her I wasn't trying to take advantage of her kindness. "Quivina... I don't want you to thin—"

"Shhh," she whispered into my mouth. "This weekend is about us feeling better for a change, even if just for a moment. We need a break from being everything and everyone, just for a little while. Let's take it... we should take every bit of what we can offer one another."

I hadn't thought of it in those terms, but she, with her sexy ass, was absolutely correct. We needed just a minute to breathe.

I decided the time for thinking about every action, analyzing every moment was done, at least until we left that room. Flipping her over onto her back, I rose up and reached into my pocket for a condom... No condom.

"I'll be right back," I growled into her mouth, angry I would have to even for a second leave the warmth of her body. The moment I left her, I may as well have been chilled to the bone.

My sleeve of condoms had fallen onto the floor, and I picked up the gold wrapper and nearly ripped the plastic into shreds getting it out. My cock was like granite as I rolled the latex onto my shaft and almost dove back across the room to her. Quivina lay there, her hand rubbing her slit slowly as she waited.

"I almost started without you," she purred.

I drank her in with my eyes, filling up on the satin sheen of her umber skin. "No, none of that. I'm here for every minute." I dropped my pants, the material hitting the floor in one fluid motion.

I wanted so badly to take it slow, to be gentle like the first time, but the sight of her with red-tipped fingernails sinking in and out of her pussy drove me into a frenzy. I leaned over her, pressing my mouth to hers and positioning myself over the apex of her thighs.

Quivina broke our kiss and ran her hand between our bodies. Her nails grazed over my flesh as they skimmed downward. When she reached my cock, the grasp of her heated hand nearly made me explode before I'd ever even reached her. I sucked in a breath, dueling against my own needs, and allowed her to guide me toward her. As I pressed into the wet heat of her body, the tight resistance of her enveloped me, and I was home.

We found our rhythm with one another, me gliding in and out of her while she stroked my back, lightly scraping her nails against my flesh.

I looked down into her eyes and leaned down to kiss her slightly open and inviting mouth. Our kiss lit fires along my senses. My body heated from within. While we only had this short weekend together, I knew she was all the things I'd denied myself for so long. Everything I'd waited for.

"Max... harder, oh God... harder, Max," she cried out.

I heard her cry, my body's reaction no different than if she'd had a hold of my reins. I was unable to think of anything other than pleasing her. Satisfying her until she forgot any pain, any sorrow from prior to that moment. I placed my hands on her hips and lifted her to increase the penetration.

She trembled and whimpered, and I watched as our bodies slammed against one another. "Quivina, I can't..." I tried to formulate thoughts, but nothing made sense beyond being inside her. I'd never felt that way with anyone before, and I didn't want it to end. If I couldn't have her after our short weekend, I would be fine forever.

My impossibly hard cock grew even harder, and I knew I wouldn't be able to hold on much longer. The thought of her not getting to have the same enjoyment as I was stopped me. I slowed my pace and pulled out of her. I could see the confusion, the protest in her eyes as she clawed at me.

I shook my head, unable to keep the smile from playing on my lips. I lowered my body, rearing back on my haunches until I was eye level with her sweet pearl. I tickled the nub with the tip of my tongue, stroking with varying intensity, hard then soft, all the way down her slit and back again. Her taste was like heaven, her scent like honey. I used my thumbs to hold her open and indulged in her until her body seized. Her thighs tightened around my head, nearly blocking out all sound, but I didn't allow the vise grip on my neck to stop me. I covered the whole of her sex with my mouth, using my tongue to lave her in my desire.

"Oh my gooddddddddd, Max," Quivina cried out once again. Her voice was ragged and hoarse, the result of screaming my name.

"You taste so good," I said, mouth still near her delicate entrance.

The bones in my neck strained against the strength of her thighs as every part of her body shuddered around me.

I didn't wait for her to stop trembling. I rose up and slid my rock-hard cock inside her, her muscles fluttering around my shaft as I pressed deeper. I thanked the Lord for her coming already because she felt so goddamn good. A second away from her sweet ecstasy would have been too much to bear. I jackhammered into her, urging my own satisfaction to come on my demand. I needed her to feel me in the same desperate way I felt her. I wanted to be one with her, in the only way I knew how.

The start of my orgasm was like a cold rain on a hot day, showering over me. Needlepoint-thin pricks of gratification ran over my body. I could have died then knowing I would never be as happy as I was at that moment.

I wanted to lie in her arms again like she had fallen asleep on me, but I knew my weight was too much. When the fine spasms of pleasure released me, I rolled onto my side and helped her get onto hers, then cradled her into my arms.

I kissed her once on the neck before moving my lips close to her ear. She needed to hear this. She needed to know. "There has never been anyone who made me feel like this before. No one."

Quivina released a coo, only a few moments passing before she murmured her agreement, followed by a soft snoring that was too cute to be anything else.

I pulled her body closer to mine and drifted off to the sound of her breaths. If I was in heaven, I prayed to God he would let me stay.

Chapter Twenty

QUIVINA

"SHOULD we go to Eastern Market for breakfast?" I asked the question as Max finished up brushing his teeth. I was seated on the edge of the bed, freshly showered from our third round of mind-blowing sex, each encounter more sensual and breathtaking than the last.

I probably could have gone another round, but the need for food not from a cart overrode my sexual thirst. I mean, I was practically a thirst trap for Max, but a girl had to eat.

"You still owe me something," he said. Max was only half dressed, and the sight of him nearly made my mouth dry out... again. He wore a pair of jeans, which I decided was my favorite look on him, with the belt, button, and zipper wide open and showing that V-shape I liked so much.

"Hmm," I replied, not quite sure of what he'd said. And pretty sure I didn't even care, if he was going to look like that.

"You were supposed to do the whole bad family comparison thing this morning. But you distracted me with your mouth… and your body… and everything. So, I showed you mine." Max had a wicked smile. That was the bad part. I was expected to walk away from him. And the worst part of it all was that it had been my idea.

"Oh… yeah. You sure you want to hear this?" I asked.

"I do. Call it quid pro quo."

"Careful with that phrase. It usually precedes something terrible. But yes. I'd like to know more about you. And if me sharing little pieces of myself with you gets me to that goal, then I'm all for it."

He raised his brows, a gentle urge for me to continue.

I took a long pause before continuing. The topic was difficult, and I hadn't ever shared it with anyone but Nell, and even with her it was limited. Max made me want to bare my soul to him. "All right. You know I was married before, like you. And in marriages, there's like this"—I couldn't help but wave my hands around as I explained—"transactional arrangement. One person negotiates how they should be treated and the other either agrees or flat-out refuses. Well, my ex-husband, Kenyon was his name, never even gave me an inch. I was to be his wife. I would take care of our home, have babies, and entertain. You ever see the movie *Stepford Wives*?"

Max took a drink of the water bottle he'd been holding and gave me a nod. "Yup," he said, after swallowing deep. His jaw ticked a bit, and I didn't know if he was angry or just listening intently. He gave another nod as if encouraging me to go on.

"So… yeah, I did that. I pushed my thoughts of teaching aside and, at my parents' encouragement, gave it all up. I thought we were on the right track, until…" I hesitated. How could I share the next detail of my raggedy marriage without breaking into a million pieces? I took a deep breath and decided maybe it was time to talk about my hardest moments. They ultimately made me who I was. And Max... well, he wouldn't be around long enough for me to have to be reminded of my lapse in judgment. "You see, in the end, I wasn't able to hold up my end of the bargain."

"What was it—you decided to go to work, after all?"

I leaned back onto the bed with my feet still dangling over the side, trying to stave off the sadness that would inevitably well up from the place in my soul where I'd locked it away. "No... that wasn't it at all. I had four miscarriages. That last time," I said, swallowing around the lump that formed in my throat, "I stayed in bed all the time, only leaving to go to the bathroom. And one of those times..." I closed my eyes, and I could still see the bright red that colored the bathroom floor and feel the searing pain in my stomach as my body rejected my last try at being a normal woman. "The doctors said I had a weak cervical floor. Sometimes women can successfully carry a baby to term and sometimes... they end up like me." I rolled onto my side, eyes still closed. I didn't want to see the pity in Max's eyes. For some reason, whenever people found out about my inability to have kids, I was never sure which emotion surfaced inside them—either they felt sorry for me or wondered what I did to contribute to the problem. Like it was my fault. At least, that's what happened when I told Kenyon. In fact, I'd screamed for him to come and help me, but he didn't come right away.

I was on the floor with my face against the ceramic tile, the only way I could cool my body. I was wracked with pain, sticky with blood, and crying from both the tragedy of losing another child and Kenyon's reaction. My heart accelerated in my chest and I panted with each involuntary contraction.

When I saw Kenyon's feet in front of my face, I tried to look up at him, but I couldn't get my body up from the floor. "He just stood there... watching me, my body rejecting the only thing I'd ever loved more than him. Then, he turned around and walked out of the room."

"He didn't..." I felt Max sit on the bed behind me, and a warm hand on my side.

"No. In fact, I lay there until the EMTs picked me up and placed me on the stretcher. But I knew... right then, more than anything I'd ever known, Kenyon was done with me. I'd known he was pulling away before, don't get me wrong, but I think he made up in his mind I was damaged."

Max shifted on the bed, and in another minute, he pulled me back into his arms. The moisture in my eyes streamed across the comforter as I moved. I hadn't even known I'd been crying. "I'm so sorry, Quivina."

"No... no, it's okay. But after that, my doctor told me I shouldn't try again. I just... I was putting my life at risk since I nearly bled out. Right there, in the bathroom. He recommended adoption, but Kenyon wouldn't hear of it."

"He sounds like a real gem of a guy."

"Tell me about it. Anyway, he decided we wouldn't have kids at all if they couldn't be his. Then, his nights at work grew longer and longer. Next thing you know, it was extended weekends. When I said something to him... he would erupt. I mean, the look in his eyes..."

I wiped at the fresh tears, then wrapped my arms around my body, trying too hard to hold the pain at bay. "He didn't look like the same person. That's when things spiraled out of control. I would try to stop him from leaving, and he would physically pick me up and hold me against the wall." I could almost still feel the burn of his handprints on my arms as he dug his fingers into my flesh. "We were toxic. I had no one to talk to. My parents thought the world of Kenyon, wouldn't believe he was capable of anything like that, and I was too embarrassed to even tell Nell.

"So I remained silent, suffering, until one day I had enough. I found an apartment and slowly furnished it with some of the money I saved from my allowance. Can you believe that shit? I was a grown-ass woman, with a PhD, and I got an allowance. Anyway, I moved out before he got home from work one day. He didn't notice for a week. I didn't tell my parents for a year. Neither did he, surprisingly. When my mother died, I came to her funeral and he was there. Still didn't say anything. Well, when I couldn't find a job, I decided to file for divorce then move back home... so I thought."

"I don't think I can imagine anything else happening. I just... I can't imagine what you must have gone through."

I shifted, pulling my legs up until I was nearly in the fetal position. "When I got here, my father wouldn't let me in his house. My savings would last me about six months, but in a hotel, it would have been much shorter. If it weren't for Nell, it would have been so much harder to get on my feet. Because of her, I have enough for a security deposit on an apartment. None of that matters to my father. We've barely spoken in weeks."

"Now, is that your choice or his?"

I rolled over onto my back and stared at the ceiling, happy I'd stopped crying, at least. "I wish I could say I was able to cut off my emotions like that, but with my mom gone and the rest of my family being in Lagos, I don't have anyone else. I didn't stop speaking to him, but every time we speak, it just dissolves into him insulting me."

Max ran a finger along my stomach and lay on his arm. I could see him watching me in my peripheral vision. "You don't deserve that," he said, his voice low and commanding.

I couldn't help the laugh that escaped. "If people only got what they deserved, the world would be a much fairer place."

"True dat."

"So, my father has a barbecue annually for his Mason friends. I thought he wouldn't do it this year, but I guess he decided to carry on with it. I'm honestly surprised he invited me. Complete with reminding me not to bring Nell. She's not his favorite."

"Why not?"

"To be honest, he doesn't have a high opinion of her because she is a lesbian. And the crowning offense, she's African American."

Max bristled. "Oh... he does that."

Not an uncommon reaction. It was something my father had often warned me about, and every time he said bad things about the few Black people from America he knew, and those he saw on television, I bristled too.

"Yeah, as much as I love my father, he can be pretty shallow. It was the reason he was so happy for me to marry Kenyon. He was a bona fide son of Nigeria and a surgeon, to boot. He called my aunties and uncles to tell them about my ex more than he ever talked about me."

Max let out something between a guffaw and a groan. "You gonna go?"

"Oh... I don't know." I didn't tell him the thought of showing up there and having to see all those disappointed men from my father's era judging me made my stomach knot. "I mean, isn't it a sign of disrespect to not go? I don't want people to think poorly of him."

"That's mighty kind of you, considering he hasn't been the kindest to you."

"He hasn't... but it'll get better." I sighed. "It has to, doesn't it?"

"Of course. I guess I have to take you to breakfast now since I ruined your morning by pressuring you to talk about that."

I turned to face him and found him staring at me, sincerity and compassion in his eyes. "Oh no, Max. I think I needed to get it out. Despite all the tears, I kind of feel better." I actually did. A little of the tension I'd been carrying around had seemed to ease.

"I'll still take you to breakfast. I could eat my own arm I'm so hungry."

"I guess we worked up an appetite," I teased.

Before I knew what was happening, Max thrust forward and kissed me full and deep on the lips. "We did, and if I could feel my legs, I'd do it again."

"That's what I get for dating an old dude."

"Hey now, I'm from the generation that created hip hop. I'm not old. We just get better."

"Sure, tell yourself that if it makes you feel better."

"I'm forty-six. Hardly a relic. Girl, I'm not defending myself against you."

"Well, I'm forty-five, so don't defend too hard. You might make me feel old too."

"We'll just leave age off the table. C'mon." He pulled me into another soft kiss. "I want to spend our last full day together showing you off."

I flushed as the words left his lips. I wish it was just from flattery, but the sinking sensation in my chest wouldn't let go. I would have to accept it. Max and I had this short time, and with the way things were with our families, there was no good reason to delude myself.

No matter how much I wanted to believe something else.

Chapter Twenty-One

MAX

"YOU BROUGHT ME TO CHURCH?" Quivina's eyes squinted in my direction.

I had to stifle my laugh and grabbed her hand to lead her up the centuries-old stairs to the high-polish doors. "Not just any church. This is a stop on the Underground Railroad. This was called the Midnight Stop for slaves but to everyone else, it was *just* a church."

Her smile was so bright, I noticed slight dimples and the way her eyes lit from within. Even the shining July sun paled in comparison.

As I opened the door for her and waited until she stepped through, I could see the upturned corners of her mouth. I hadn't taken a woman out in a while, but I knew what it all meant... she was surprised. Maybe it would be presumptive to add pleasantly surprised, but she did look intrigued.

"Do I get to tour the Underground Railroad today?" The smile morphed into a smirk on her lips.

"Not just any tour," I replied as mysteriously as I could manage. I was relieved by her excitement, since I'd spent most of the morning trying to come up with the perfect date for her. It was the least I could do after dragging her through so many bad memories. Well, maybe for me, as well. I needed a respite from all the crazy things happening in my life. Between my sister's ongoing illness topped off by helping her with the kids, there wasn't much time for anything else. I was thankful to Smith, even if he was pissed at me, for taking the kids so I could get this much-needed adult time. As we walked into the sanctuary, Pastor Jay Cleese was waiting for us near the altar.

"Good afternoon, Pastor Jay," I called out to him. My portly friend was wiping down the front pews of the church. There were people to do that for him, but he was of the mindset that cleaning and service to others kept a person humble.

"Brother Maxwell. Good afternoon," He neatly folded the bright yellow towel and placed it on the end of the pew. He wiped his hands on a clean white handkerchief after extracting it from his pocket. "Good to see you." He extended his hand while walking toward us.

I shook his hand, then pulled my girl closer to me. "This is my friend and colleague, Quivina Adedeji. Quivina, this is Pastor Cleese, but he'll tell you—"

"I tell people that was my father and he was a far better Cleese than me. A pleasure to meet you." He gently grasped her hand in his. "I'm glad you could come by today." He gave her a warm smile, which she returned in kind.

True, he was a pastor and one of my oldest friends, but something lurched inside my chest when Jay took Quivina's hand. The cold sensation of possession snaked over me, even if she wasn't *mine* or some other primal shit that still plagued men even post-evolution. "Do you need us to give you a few moments before we get started?"

"Oh no. I was just keeping my hands busy. I finished my sermon and while I'm not the"—holding up his hands, he made air quotes—"*official* conductor of this tour, I've been on it several times. Anyway, Max you know way more about history than anyone I've ever met. If the Conservation Society wouldn't kill me, I'd let you two go it alone. And FYI, I'm not even joking about the killing me part. They are serious about the Midnight Stop." He laughed.

"You don't have to tell me," I agreed, the knot of tension from Jay holding her hand easing as I joked with the man.

"Before I forget," Jay said, pointing a finger at me, "I was told to ask if you were going to join the Society this year. Again. I said I would mention it."

If I wasn't in church, I probably would have cursed. "Interesting. If they were actually doing some work to preserve Detroit's gems, I would consider it. Could you relate that to them for me?" I said, unable to keep the edge out of my tone.

"Easy there, old friend. I'm just passing along the request. I'll tell them and then I'll give them your info so they can do their own dirty work." The rich notes of Jay's voice bounced along the ceiling beams in the highest arches of the building.

"Can we please get on with impressing this nice lady so she'll go out with me again?" I pulled Quivina's hand into mine once more. She made me way happier than I'd been in a long time, even if she wasn't going to be around to make me feel that way for long.

"Right away, man. Quivina, do you have a nickname or something you prefer to go by?" Jay asked.

Quivina blinked once, but if there was any annoyance

there, it wasn't immediately visible. "My friends call me Q," she said, her voice even and crisp.

"Q it is. I'm going to grab my keys and meet you in the back of the church, just through that doorway, okay? Be right back." He turned and half jogged down the aisle.

When he was out of earshot, I turned to Quivina again. "See that? Lazy tongue, like I said."

Quivina's eyes narrowed for a moment before widening with realization. Then she smiled, a wide, bright curve of her lips to reveal spectacularly white teeth. "You are aware we're in a church, right?"

"Oh, this is where I do some of my best dirty jokes. Although, I'm not sure why your mind is in the gutter. Tongues aren't inherently sexy, are they?" I feigned innocence, but the veil, if there at all, was threadbare and nearly completely transparent.

"Let's go. I'm pretty sure I won't win this argument." She tugged her hand free from mine, slapping me on the forearm, then turning in the direction of the door.

Quivina was all graceful elegance and ample curves wrapped in silken brown skin. But while I liked the way she looked, her wit and intellect were what had me following behind her like a little puppy dog hoping for a scratch behind the ear. If I were to think on it, there hadn't been a woman to call me on my shit in years. That wasn't surprising because it certainly wasn't a woman's job to straighten dudes out.

I'd gotten a look at the rest of her, complete with her heavenly scent when we were in my car on the way over to the church. The women in my life were all fiery like that, and she reminded me of my mother and sister. They never took my bull, nor let me slide with it. I think I liked that character trait most of all.

It didn't take Jay long to get the tour underway. He took

us into the underbelly of the church, navigating all the stairs and corridors of the historically preserved passages—even the walls were veritable keepers of African American history, and she soaked it up.

I was enamored with her very spirit. Even if she'd heard all the stories or been on one of the slave routes before, she was enthralled, and everything about her came to life—from her eyes to her hands moving along the unprotected spaces to feel the same spaces as people desperate to find their freedom. She was the first person I'd shared the space with, and I was sincerely thankful to have experienced it with her.

When we were done with the tour, after thanking Pastor Jay, we moved on to the restaurant—another Detroit gemstone called Motor City Blues Café. All the way there, she entertained me with happier stories about her family, her time on the West Coast, and finally, her journey back home. I nearly forgot about everything else, including all the worries over my sister.

"I feel like I've been jabbering away for hours. So, tell me something about your childhood memories. We only know the bad stuff." She added a heavy emphasis on the word *bad*.

She was attuned to me, her body slightly leaning forward, one hand lingering on the cocktail straw of her margarita and the other arm outstretched on the table before her as if she were studying my movements. Active listening was rumored to exist but very few people employed it.

I knew this to be factual since I stood in front of semi-adults multiple times weekly with the hopes that just one would assume Quivina's exact position. Very few did, unless I was teaching graduate level and even then, they were only partially engaged.

Quivina's non-judgmental, gently encouraging presence allowed me to drop the guard of pretense I'd always needed to carry. It was a salve to all my past hurts, a buoy in the turbulent waves of my soul.

"Well, there's not much to know. Before I moved in with my dad, my mom would take me to museums and libraries almost every weekend. We got on great, even though it was just the two of us. You know, she and my dad didn't work out. But my mom used to say when she was reminiscing that I had his temper and his smile."

"I'm sorry for your loss, Max." She leaned forward a bit more to stroke a soft hand over the flesh of my forearm.

"It's okay, but thank you. It was years ago when she passed. I moved in with my father and then I had a new stepmom and siblings. It was so new and... can I say something without sounding corny?"

"Oh please, give me all the corny. I love that shit."

"Yeah, yeah... well"—I leaned back in the chair and inhaled deeply—"it was the first time I had a nuclear family, so after the fog of my mother's death, I was finally part of a family. It stayed that way for years, until..."

"Until your father's death?"

"And the accident. My stepmother passed about five years after all that went down. And I felt like it was my responsibility to take care of Cami and Smith. So—"

"And that's why you worry about your siblings, and your nieces and nephews, the way you do."

I felt the clog in my throat. It was all too much, and I wasn't sure why I kept pouring my soul out to her. "You know what? You asked for happy memories, so every Valentine's Day, my dad and stepmom would give us hearts. They'd cut this red construction paper up—"

"Oh, like in elementary school, how awesome."

"I know right? They'd attach them to a big bag of candy. They always said *to our loves of our lives*. It was really sweet.

They gave them to us every Valentine's Day for as long as they lived."

"So sweet." She clasped her hands together and brought them in to her chest.

"And there you have it. That was who my parents were, all three of them."

"Well, I'd say you're a very blessed man, even though they left you too soon."

I raised my glass in her direction. Quivina touched her cocktail glass to the lip of mine. "To everyone who left us too soon," I said.

"Cheers to them," she said before taking a drink.

I swallowed a big gulp of my cognac and set it on the table. "So, what do you want to do now? Maybe I could show you the People Mover or we can stroll on the River Walk?" I waited for her response, but she was just staring at me as if she was torn between whether to answer my question or say something else.

"Tomorrow is supposed to be the end. And everything is supposed to be out of our systems, but..."

"Yeah." I took a deep breath. Honestly, she made me feel incredible, and I hadn't felt that way in so long, I didn't even want to think about Monday. Because I knew it would be over.

"I decided I'm going to my father's party. And I want you to go with me," she said in a rush.

"I'm pretty sure I'm the last person your father wants to meet, given his thoughts about my nationality."

"I know... I just thought I would give it a shot. You make me feel better, and I thought it would be nice to feel better while I'm there." She sat back in her chair and shook her head. I could see the regret on her face at my rejection.

"Quivina, the last thing I want to do is cause you any more trouble. But I don't want to lie to my brother about...

hell, about anything. And with him feeling the way he's feeling, I just... I just don't see how we can go beyond this weekend." The words were like knives coming out of my mouth, but I needed to do this for Smith. He deserved better after all the pain I'd caused him.

"I know... I know. I'm sorry I asked. I just thought..."

"And I need you to know, if things were any other way, I would have gone with you to that party and turned it out, you hear me?" I chortled, hoping to lighten up the mood.

But she wasn't buying it. "You know, Max... you're right. It was foolish of me to think that we could do this."

"Wait a minute, that's not what I meant at all. We're having a great weekend an—"

"I'm not this girl, you know?" Quivina placed her napkin on the table and began to stand. "I have no practice with casual sex, and I thought I could be more like... more like someone else." She stood up fully. "I'm not able to keep things compartmentalized like this. And it's not your fault, but I shouldn't have done any of this." She turned to walk away, and I practically leapt out of my seat.

"Just wait a minute. I'm not upset about anything that happened. I just don't want to... we can't just go on like no one has been hurt here. Smith must have really liked you, and I don't want to hurt him." I was in front of her before she could leave the table, holding on to her arms because something told me if she walked away, I would regret it for the rest of my life.

"But I'm still too broken to start something with anyone. I wasn't ready. Not even to start dating. It was a bad idea I let my friend talk me into it. And when I saw her with her girlfriend, I think I just got jealous and wanted to feel that way about someone again. I enjoyed this too, but obviously, it's just too much."

Before I could respond, the waiter came back over to the table. "Are you guys taking off?"

I glanced back to the guy, who must have thought we were about to dine and dash. "No."

"Yes," Quivina cut in.

"Here." I pulled my wallet from my back pocket and handed a credit card to him.

As he accepted it, I felt Quivina brush past me.

"I'll get this right back to you, sir," the waiter told me, then walked briskly from the chaos.

I couldn't think about my card, choosing instead to run behind Quivina, who was almost to the front door. I took off, but before I could get two steps, I ran into a server carrying a basket of bread and a glass of wine.

Bread flew across the room and the wine spilled over both of us. As the girl stumbled back, I caught her before she could hit the ground.

Once I apologized, the red wine scent filling my nose, Quivina was gone. I stepped out onto the street to look but it was too late. She'd disappeared into the night.

And fuck me, if that didn't hurt like a knife in the heart.

Chapter Twenty-Two

"OH MY GOD, where have you been? I called you four times this weekend," Nell scolded.

I was already at the table having some of her overnight oats for breakfast. "Oh, I'm sorry. I was... I was with Max." Before she could get into it, I not-very-skillfully shifted topics. "So, I wanted to apologize for walking in on you and Trinity like that."

Nell's brows knitted as she studied me. She knew very well I was running game but quickly shifted into friend mode. "It's okay, it's fine. I wish I wouldn't have put you in that position, but we were okay."

"No, I'm a huge inconvenience to you, and I am looking for a place I can afford, so I'll be out of here as soon as possible."

"Girl." Nell walked over and took a seat at the small kitchen table beside me. "I don't want you to leave. I'll just have to relegate my date nights to the bedroom. That's all." She gave me a smile and ran a hand over my forearm.

"I still feel so shitty about it. And then..." I started to tell her about my rash decision to sleep with Max, but I didn't even know how to start.

"You slept with Max."

I started once to lie, but my mouth was wide open, surely giving me away. "It was all so..."

"It's the comfort effect."

"The what?"

"The comfort effect. Sometimes, when we're single and see another couple canoodling, we go seek out comfort."

"I'm pretty sure that's not a thing."

"Oh, it is. I've slept with so many people at weddings because of it." Nell held up both hands and wiggled her fingers with a snort. "Is there any coffee?"

"Yup, in the pot." I pointed over my shoulder to the counter. "While I don't believe you, that pretty much happened. I was downstairs waiting for you guys to um..."

"Finish up?" Nell's brows popped. She gave me jazz hands and walked over to pour her cup of coffee.

"Y-yes. So I went down to Max's to wait and we were talking about his ex and one thing led to another... and we were kissing." I ran a hand over my hair and down to the side of my neck, a feeble attempt to mimic his touch. The thought of Max's hands on me forced a flash of heat over my body. I couldn't even look at Nell as she came back to the table and took the seat in front of me. Instead, I concentrated on the window and not looking at any one thing, since the real goal was avoidance.

"It happens. But what about Smith? I mean, we talked about you not dating anyone, then you suddenly shift brothers? There's a lot more to this story... it's not like you just fell onto his lips?"

"No, I didn't fall on his mouth. But however it happened, the end result was Smith walking in on us."

Nell made a quick air-sucking noise as I explained everything that had happened. To her credit, she didn't ask any questions. She just listened, something I hadn't even known I needed.

"Oh."

I gave her a nod to let her know it was just as bad as the expression on her face. "I know. So, he exploded on Max, naturally. And me, but I'm more concerned about their relationship. I mean, I'm just a woman you know? Disposable almost. What is it they say, bros before hos?"

Nell reached a hand outward and waved it in my direction. "You aren't disposable. And you most definitely aren't a ho. No one slit-shames my best friend. Even you. You went on a few dates with Smith. You weren't exclusive. And sometimes, things happen that maybe we should have done in another way. But you aren't the root cause of all their problems. You understand me?"

I gave her a smile, knowing she was doing what any good bestie would by being on my side. "You don't understand. They have a lot of problems, and you're right, they aren't all about me. But the truth is, Max isn't going to choose me over his brother. I can't really say I wouldn't do the same for a sibling or a friend. You know? Anyway, I had this grand idea to spend a weekend with him to get it out of my system."

"Lemme guess. Epic failure?"

"Oh girl, I had a breakdown yesterday and came home, locked myself in the room, and didn't sleep a wink. So, yes… that about sums it up." I bit my lip to keep the tears from falling. The worst part was I didn't even know why I was crying, exactly.

Nell took the coiled band off her wrist and pulled all her curls into a ball as she spoke. "You know, it's okay to mess up sometimes."

"I know, but I think I mess up most of the time. I think..." I started, unsure how to tell her the rest. I resolved in the narrow space of time that I needed to start talking about my feelings, how others made me feel. I'd spent too long hiding behind what others told me I should be doing and not enough time on what I wanted for myself. "I got a little jealous of... of you and Trinity. You know, it's stupid right?"

"Oh honey," she said.

"I mean, you should be in a relationship and happy, I just wanted to grab a little of that for myself. For once."

Nell leaned over the table, her arms wide and extended. I leaned in to give her an awkward, yet kind and warm hug. "Girl, I wish I could tell you I'm happy all the time. The truth is, I'm not. Trinity and I were okay when you... when you saw us the other day, but the truth is, I think I'm falling for her. And I don't know how to do that, Q."

"Oh Nell." I pulled out of her grasp to look at her. "Why didn't you tell me?"

Nell sat back in her chair and rolled her eyes before focusing on me once again. "Honestly?"

"Yeah, honestly." Concern burned into my stomach. I didn't want to have a one-sided relationship with Nell. She was my oldest friend and we needed to be there for one another, no matter what. I focused in on her deep brown eyes, my face tight with worry.

"Well, you have a lot going on, and I didn't want to burden you with my troubles. But the main reason I didn't tell you was your inability to understand same-sex relationships. I always get the feeling that you don't necessarily believe that this is who I am. Like it's a phase or something."

"Nell." I grabbed at my T-shirt, trying to loosen the neck. It felt like my air was being cut off. "I know this isn't a phase. I've never even thought such a thing. What would make you think that?"

"We didn't get a chance to talk after... well, you walked in and saw everything... And I'm not sure I would have been ready even if you were here. But aside from all that, you know you didn't have to leave."

"I want—I wanted to give you some space. I thought Trinity would be here. And since I didn't know if she was staying there, I thought you didn't want me to know... I mean, not that you had to, but I didn't understand why you didn't tell me... Did you think I would judge you?" For the first time, there was tension between us. It was unusual, and I don't think Nell liked it any more than I did.

"You mean...?" She held her head down. I could see the relief seeping in as her shoulders relaxed. "You didn't understand why I didn't tell you I was with a woman? I want to say something brave like love is love and... all that other stuff. But the truth is, I didn't know how you would react. And if it went badly, I didn't know if I was ready to face a world without you in it."

"Oh my, God... no. I think you're one of the most brilliant people I know, beautiful, kindhearted, fierce, and a walking IMDB. And the person you love is a woman. It's just another part of who you are. Nell, I'm probably saying this really poorly, but I'm just trying to express that you're my best friend. And one day, if you pick someone, I'm going to be your maid of honor or best woman at your wedding. You tell me what you want, and I'll be there, every time." By the time I finished, my eyes were blurry with tears. The thought of me not accepting her... the whole time I'd been worried that she wasn't accepting me. "You have your entire life together, and I'm just happy to be a part of it all."

I stared over at her, her hands clutched over her heart. "I

was so scared… so afraid I'd lose you like the rest of my family. Knowing is one thing, but seeing is—"

"Listen, Nell, it's always embarrassing for everyone to see sex they aren't involved in. But the real truth is, beyond my own envy of your happiness, I thought it was all too much for you. Me not exactly being open with you for years, then barging into your home. Like, you can't even have any private time."

"Girl, that's okay…"

"No, let me tell you. I held some things back from you —well, because I was embarrassed. Kenyon was verbally and physically abusive to me when we were together. I didn't tell you, and I felt so alone. I didn't have any of my own friends in Atlanta. I thought they'd get too close to me and find out. That someone would see the cracks in my crystal. It was horrible. I was horrible…"

"Oh Q. I'm so sorry. And you are not horrible. He is, for trying to snuff out your light."

"I let him—"

"No, he did this. You were a victim. He held all the power. I just wish you'd felt like you could have talked to me."

"Nell, I didn't want you to get caught up in my shit. I dealt with it. Actually"—I let out a pitiful laugh—"he was already gone long before I left. And then, I told my father. You know what he said?"

Nell, with a tragic expression on her face, only shook her head and dabbed at my cheeks with a napkin.

"He said Kenyon was under a lot of stress because I can't have kids. That I should forgive him." A fresh sob broke from my chest.

"Did you tell him he was hitting you?"

"I—maybe… I think I froze while telling him. I stopped… I thought he would blame me for it."

"Wow. How heartless can you be?"

"He's all I have left, Nell. I can't give up on him." Even as I said it, I knew if we didn't work it out, I'd have no choice but to do just that.

"I won't tell you to close the door on your relationship with your parent, but he has to learn to respect you and your needs. You respected his more than your own for so long. It's time he returned the favor."

"We'll get there. I know I have to tell him how I've felt all these years... my whole life actually. And he isn't the only person I need to talk to." I let out a sigh, then collapsed against Nell when she pulled her chair closer and placed one arm around me.

"Are you gonna speak to Max?"

"No... I don't think he's the person I need to deal with first. I mean, as good as he makes me feel, I didn't hurt him. No, I have to go through my own little bit of healing, one person at a time."

"Well, you may need to turn your cell off. It's been vibrating on your dresser all morning."

"Yeah, I know." I sat up, straightened my shoulders, and grabbed my own napkin from the dispenser on the table. "I know. But a lot of this happened because I was only looking inward. It's time to get a little stronger. If I don't do that, I continue to only accept what others are willing to give me. Not what I actually want. I can't live like that anymore."

"Okay, queen. But don't ever again think I won't understand something you're going through. You're the person who reached into the closet and pulled me out, remember? I'll always have your back."

"I've got yours too, Nell. Forever. But um... let's use the sock-on-the-doorknob method going forward."

"How about we text when we're bringing someone over? Jesus, this isn't 1975, for fuck's sake."

"Deal," I said.

I spent the rest of the morning filling Nell in on so many of my life's darkest moments, and I felt better than I had in a long time.

Chapter Twenty-Three

MAX

I'D NEVER BEEN BLOCKED before. It was an interesting thing. Once I'd gotten a divorce, I was sure my women problems were over for the rest of my life. I'd sworn to myself everything would be casual going forward. No serious entanglements, especially where women were concerned. Unless I was related to a lady by blood, I didn't want anything beyond momentary flings.

Shit. I sat in the hospital parking structure instead of waiting in my apartment for Quivina's call because my sister had asked me to meet her at the hospital for a family meeting. As much as I loved Cami, after so many months trying to ensure she was okay, I wanted to be somewhere else. With *Quivina*.

After four days, she probably wasn't going to call anyway.

I finally dragged my ass to my sister's room, even though it meant I would have to face my shitty situation. I wasn't extremely surprised to see Smith there, along with the kids.

Cami had promised me it wasn't a life-or-death emergency, but the look on her face was grim when I walked in. In fact, they all had the same look of seriousness. "Hey big bro, we've been waiting." Her voice was ragged and hoarse like she'd been yelling at someone.

One look at Smith, and I knew who. "What's the deal?" I asked.

"I didn't snitch, Uncle Max," Diane blurted out before Smith or Cami could reply. "It was Donnie. He told—"

"Shut up, Di. It was a matter of family security. I was within my rights to bring in an authority figure."

"Mom isn't even the oldest," she snapped.

"Hey, hey. Donnie, don't tell your sister to shut up," I said. "And you, Diane, there's no such thing as snitching. We tell our truths even when we're afraid or feel like we're getting someone we care about in trouble. If anyone does something that hurts you, you'd better tell one of us, you understand?"

"Yeah, I hear you, Uncle Max," she said, barely audible.

"I'm not mad at you guys. Right now, I actually need a pop. Can you two go down to the machine in the lounge and grab me a Coke?" I fished a five out of my billfold and handed it to Donnie, who was at my side immediately.

"Yes. Uncle Smith, you want anything?"

Smith hadn't uttered a word since I'd been in the room, until then. "No, buddy. I'm good."

"Okay." Donnie turned around to grab his sister's sleeve. "C'mon Di. They're going to yell some more."

"Be good, kids, and come right back in here." Cami leaned to the side to see around my frame that blocked the door.

"Yes, ma'am," the twins yelled back.

Once their footsteps were faint and the hiss of the door

softly closing stopped, Cami turned to me, then to Smith. "Alright. Wanna tell me what's going on? Donnie said you two aren't speaking. Smith, the kids told me you insinuated that Max hurt you in the accident and walked away without even caring how your life was affected. What kind of thing is that to say in front of my kids?"

Smith turned away from her and stared at the closed bathroom door. "I didn't mean it, okay. I was just pissed. That he couldn't tell me he wanted Q. She wasn't even my girl."

"I wasn't going to act on it... I wouldn't have, but both you and she said you were just friends. I had every intention of leaving her alone."

"Then why didn't you?"

"Okay," Cami cut in. "The kids will be back in a moment, and I need to say this. Whatever you two have going on with this lady, and I'm sure she's lovely, I need you. I'm not well. I trusted you to take care of my kids, and until I'm better, you'll have to co-parent in my absence. It shook them to see you two go after one another. When you add your rift to my sickness, neither of those children feel safe. Now if this is too much for you, I can and will send them to stay with their father's mom while he's deployed an—"

"Not an option," Smith said.

"Absolutely not. We've seen the son she raised," I added.

"Well, y'all are not giving me any choices here. I need you to do better. Can you?" Cami still looked small, her body a fraction of its normal size. But her eyes were on fire, the look of determination that could only belong to a mother.

"I didn't mean what I said. I was angry, that's all. I just need time to get past it. The kids don't have to be worried," Smith said.

"But you don't get it. There's no time out when you're caring for children. I need you to both behave. That means walking the walk and showing you care about them. If you need to argue or fight or anything else, you do it when the kids aren't around. No more dropping them off at the door, no more sending messages through them. You want to talk to one another, you pick up your damn phones and call or text, like adults. My kids are not your messengers. And it makes them nervous. Understand?" Cami used her arms to sit up straight on the hospital bed and pulled a string to turn on the light above her. It was getting dark outside and the dim glow lit the room alongside the setting sun.

"I understand." I didn't want to cause her any stress. My sister didn't deserve that.

"I'm able to speak to him. We'll take care of the kids, Cami." Smith shifted in the chair that was way too small for his broad frame.

"Nope, I said you need to be believable. Smith, you can't even look at him," she scolded. "I need you guys to go into the family room down the hall and grill that beef you have. Don't come out until you have some goddamn common sense." Cami looked from one of us to the other, her pointed finger following her eyes.

"I don't think that's necessary, Cami. We understand," I said.

"Nope. You take your asses down to that room and don't come back until you can calmly explain to me and the kids which house they're sleeping at tonight."

I wanted to protest more, but she wasn't having it. She looked just like our father when he had on his "you've done it now" face.

Smith stood up and walked past me, his shoulder bumping mine.

The bump jolted me, but I didn't react. Instead, I looked to my sister, who just narrowed her eyes and shook her head, the two plaits on either side shaking back and forth with her movement. "Alright. I'll fix it."

"I can't do this without you guys, Max. You like taking care of people, so take care of me."

I couldn't even respond. I just gave her a nod I hoped was reassuring and followed the same path as Smith. I walked past the nurse's station, a crew of women who looked like they'd be glad when the shift changed. I gave them a nod too, since we both had seen better days.

I found Smith in a room near the end of the fluorescent-lit hallway. I walked in and took the chair nearest him.

"I'm sorry." The words came out in a rush, but I meant it.

"Yeah, well… maybe if you would have spoken to me in the first place, we wouldn't be in this situation."

"You're probably right about that." I leaned onto the table and turned to look at him over my shoulder. "I think you already know I don't always make the best decisions."

"Tell me about it."

"But you know I never meant to hurt you. Not back then, and certainly not now. What you said, man…"

"I didn't mean it. It just—"

"Smith, it hit home. I made a promise to our father on his deathbed I'd take care of you and Cami forever. I've always made every effort to keep my promise to him. It's the least I can do."

Smith leaned back in the chair and scrubbed his hands over his face. "I know you think you need to take care of us. But I'm not fragile. Cami may not be at one hundred percent, but however she comes out of here, she won't need someone to pity her. She'll need her brother. We have been letting you work off this penance you took on after the accident because we knew you were hurting. But the time has come for us to be adults."

"I know that. But, you can't just turn off your primary directive when you've been following it for twenty years. I don't want to let you down again, know what I mean?"

"You are misconstruing what I'm saying. I'm not saying change who you are. I'm saying stop trying to control everything. You can't. People have free will and things they want from life that have nothing to do with you. If I get hurt, then I just do. Same with Cami. But my problem is, as close as you claim we are, you could have said you were attracted to Q. And maybe we would have had some words, but I can't help who someone wants. I just thought we were better than this."

"And we are."

"Then telling me shouldn't have been that hard. But you didn't. Instead, I walked in and saw someone I thought was interested in me with your tongue down her throat and your hands on her ass. That's a fucking mess, man."

For a moment, I was stricken, unable to form the words when he laid out how raggedy I'd been toward him when only the promise of her sweet kiss was presented. As he explained it to me using such plain words, I understood that my course of action should have been to resist. To talk to him. To tell my brother that I had feelings for Quivina. I didn't even love her yet, but one day with her and I'd known she would be something to me. It had been so long, I hadn't even recognized those feelings. "I should have come to you first, and for that, I'm so sorry. I want to tell you I regret everything. But I don't. I like Quivina. Like, a lot. But I should not have acted on it without telling you."

"Have you been with her... intimately?"

My first thought was to lie. I worked out the explanation in my mind and was set to tell him a resounding no. "Yes," came out instead. "We were together. It was supposed to be once. And it has been. But she's the only person I've ever been able to take into all my dark corners. You know what I mean?"

"No, actually." Smith sat up too at that moment. He leaned on his elbows beside me on the table. "I've never shared anything like that with anyone. Not even Q. So, no. I haven't been to the mountain you speak of. But I understand."

I was so greedy, I wanted him to say he forgave me. Sensibility stopped me, however. "It felt so good. But, I should tell you, I don't think she'll see me again. I haven't spoken to her since Saturday. I've been a mess. I've called her and... I, uh..." I floundered to back out of my admission. I was sure Smith didn't want to know about my troubles with her. "Thank you though, for keeping the kids this week. I don't want them to see me like this. Sometimes, I just sit and stare into space."

"Have you gone to see her?" he asked even though it must have still been a sore spot.

"No. That's kind of toxic, you know? I think I've messed things up pretty good."

"She called me. And then when I wouldn't answer, she came to see me at work."

"What?" A spike of pain hit the center of my chest. I wanted to be the one she reached for when she was sad. "When?"

"Yesterday. She told me about what happened. Said she was sorry for her part in the situation. And I told her it was fine." He smiled for the first time, a sly one that didn't light his face like his smiles usually did. "And I appreciate what you tried to do, but I'm all good. If you and Q want to make a go of it, you should."

"Oh."

"I think you two probably need to speak, though. You're never going to get to the bottom of whether this is something you really want if you don't talk to one another. I'm not in the way."

"So... she didn't mislead you?" While I was restating the obvious, it was primarily a relief to hear aloud. I hadn't even known that was a concern, but coupled with Smith's reaction, I needed to hear the admission.

"We talked about that, and the truth is, we vibed more as friends. At the time, I did believe that, but you know... when I saw you, I realized everything she'd done was for you." Smith shifted away from me, his body stiff with whatever thoughts were left unsaid.

For a moment, I couldn't say anything. A part of me still held on to the guilt over the way things had played out. I knew there was only one way around that, and that was to level with him. "I know I was selfish. I didn't want you to be hurt, but I also wanted her. This won't ever be enough of an apology, but it's the truth."

"You know, the truth is medicine."

"I guess."

"It's medicine that may taste bad, but now that I have it, it made me feel better. So, thank you for explaining that to me."

"You're welcome."

"And for the record, I forgave you by Monday. But I was embarrassed by all the things I said to you. I don't blame you for the accident. There have been feelings of anger, and I should have talked to you about them... you know, my therapist warned me it was going to come out badly one day if I didn't control the narrative."

"I get it. And since we're on the topic, I never forgave myself for ending your career. You were going to be a star, and one bad decision on my part ended that. And our father's life."

"He was going to have a heart attack anyway, Max."

I couldn't look back to my brother even though I felt the weight of his stare on the side of my face. "It wa—"

"It was the eighty-five percent blockage coupled with a stressful situation. He had high blood pressure from years of eating badly and not working out. It was the perfect cocktail for the worst possible outcome. Not your fault."

I ran a hand over my face and let it fall to my lap. Smith wasn't telling me anything new. I saw the autopsy report, I knew what the doctors said, and I knew what Evelyn, my stepmother had told me again and again. But it was the first time I heard one of my siblings completely absolve me of any wrongdoing. And I needed it. The weight of the last twenty years lifted from my back, and I could finally breathe. I took a deep breath and turned to face Smith fully. "Thank you, man."

Smith nodded and placed a hand on my arm, gently giving it a squeeze. "You always try very hard to take care of us. We know what you're doing. You don't have to be our dad anymore. We can stand on our own two feet now," he said, a coarse rattle in his voice.

I blinked hard to hold back tears. "I'm supposed to be apologizing to you."

"And you have, every day since the accident. It's time we cut you some slack. You deserve to be happy. Have a relationship. Start a family again, but this time, give it your whole heart. You haven't been able to do that, from what I can tell. You left your soul back in 2002."

"I'm not that bad, dog."

"You are. I'm surprised you were able to get that lady to

marry you. Whatever you do, don't mess up with Q." Smith's brows screwed down tight as he finished the sentence—the one he saved for capping on me like when we were children. "She might be your last chance considering you didn't get the looks in the family." He ended with a harder-than-necessary punch on the shoulder.

"Oh, it's like that? We're on me even though you dress like a dejected rapper?"

"Aww, dog… here we go. Gone now, before I change my mind and take all the girls." He offered up a sardonic smile.

"You probably could, beefcake. But for real, we're good, right? Because I… I love you, bro." I stopped with the jokes because I meant it. Smith and my family meant more to me than anyone. I wasn't extremely vocal, but he needed to understand why his forgiveness was so important to me.

"I love you too, man." He leaned over and gave me a one-armed hug, which I reciprocated. "But for real, fix that shit with Q. She's kind, and you should go with her to the barbeque."

I let go of him then. "She told you about that?"

"Believe it or not, we're friends. Always have been. Just because I get mad at someone doesn't mean I write them off. Yes. She told me you turned her down because of me. And as much as I appreciate the gesture, I think you need to rectify that by taking her."

"Her father doesn't like us, though. I don't know if I should go."

"It's your chance to help her through something really hard for her. As uncomfortable as you may be, some things are worth it."

I leaned forward on my elbows and pondered the situation for a moment. "I'll ask her again… tomorrow."

"Why not tonight?"

"I think it should be face-to-face, and tomorrow is one

of the Inspiration Alley events we've been planning. And I should talk to her in person."

"Alright, but don't wimp out. She's worth fighting for."

"Don't I know it, bro." He was right. I knew I should have fought in the first place.

Chapter Twenty-Four

QUIVINA

THE DAYS LEADING up to the 360Project's next Inspiration Alley event went by at a snail's pace. My heart had been through the meat grinder essentially. It physically hurt to block Max's calls.

"So, you and Smith, or what's his nickname—"

"Pronto, but I'm not calling him that anymore."

"Okay, well Smith, then. You guys are good, and you're ready to take on the next challenge. I feel like you're on a mission, girl." Nell grinned as she slid a slice of her frittata toward me. "You know what I want?"

"What's..." I took a bite of the most fabulous thing to happen to eggs and returned my attention to her. "What's that?"

"I will fully expect leftover jollof rice since I can't go to your dad's event this weekend."

"It's gonna be a hot-ass mess, girl." I took a sip of my orange juice and gave her a look of sorrow.

"I would go if you needed me to. I swear."

"I do need support, but it's not fair of me to drag you into this mess. I'm going to be telling him he can't be judgmental anymore and that I am going to go out, live my best life, and he can either come with me or he won't have to worry about disowning me. I'm going to disown him."

"Wow." Nell nodded her head. "Okay, girl. It's about time."

"Damn right." I tried my hardest to give her a mean mug, furrowing my brows, and took an aggressive bite of my breakfast.

Nell chortled so hard she nearly spit out her orange juice. "You're... you're gonna just go in hard like that?"

"I am." I giggled and continued eating, but I knew it wasn't going to be as easy as I'd made it out to be. My stomach grew tighter, but I refused to let fear drive me anymore.

"And what about Max? Are you ready to talk to him yet?"

"I don't know... like, for a second, I was basing my happiness on a man. Another one. I felt myself slipping. I'm not ready to do that again. So, I think I need to get myself together. Let me lose ten pounds first." I ran my finger around the rim of my glass before taking a sip. Just saying the words aloud, for the first time, took the onus from my father and Kenyon, and ultimately Max, and placed it back on my shoulders, where it should have been in the first place.

"Okay, I hear that too."

"Yeah, it's what's best. You know."

"I do. Did you ever listen to his voicemails?"

It was a what, seven-word question, and it made my heart sink. "No... no, I didn't. I'm not ready. I blocked his calls from my phone, and haven't really looked at them yet." I knew why too. But I wasn't ready to share that just yet. I knew in my heart if I heard his voice I would cave. He was too good to be true. He made my heart flutter and parts of me awaken. In such a short time, I'd come to need him. I couldn't afford to need him so much.

"I'm going to tell you something. I razzed you about being with someone, but I shouldn't have. Totally the right move to get your head on straight. And the timing was so very shitty to meet Max. But... you gotta ask yourself this question. Were you happy with him? And yeah, it wasn't for the longest time—it was maybe a few days—but did he make you smile? There's no rush on this, so don't think that's what I'm trying to get you to do. But I am asking that you give him a chance when you're where you need to be. Don't punish yourself for your past. You thought you were doing the right thing with Ken. Sometimes, the people we loved just weren't our forever person. Don't throw out someone who is good because you are afraid of being hurt again. Otherwise, no one would ever do anything."

Her words washed over me. She was right. Without me even saying anything, she knew I was scared. "I love you, girl. You keep it real all the time. I'll think about it." Nell gave me a sideways look. "I swear."

"Go listen to his messages, at least. I won't pressure you to call him. I've told you that, but I do know how hard it is to find real love. I can speak from experience. When I met Trinity, she was the very last thing I was looking for. And she has slowly become... I'm going to ask her to marry me... And I want that for you." Her voice cracked, and I knew those last beautiful words about Trinity were real.

"What? Did you just sa—"

"Yes, girl. I want to marry that woman. She is so..."

"I haven't even met her yet. I mean, I met her, but not—"

"Okay, girl. I know what you mean." Nell smiled, her fair cheeks burning red.

"Why didn't you tell me?"

She shrugged her shoulders. "I mean, you're going through so much. So, so much. I just didn't want to make you feel like my life was taking off when you were dealing with so many things. That was my bad."

"Come here." I rose from the table, extending my arms. Nell stood and met me in the middle. I wrapped my arms around her, pulling her in. As we met, I kissed her on the cheek. "I love you so very much. This is the best thing in the world, and I will never begrudge you happiness just because I'm not as happy."

"I love you too, Q. You are my girl, and I will always stand behind you. Don't walk away from happiness because you are afraid."

I felt her hand run over my hair and in her kindness and love, I fell apart. For what I hoped was the last time.

Then I went back to my room and sat on the edge of the bed, holding my phone on my lap. I opened the voicemail screen and pressed the button to hear my messages. The first one was the last—and it moved me.

"By this point, I know you aren't listening. I reacted badly, but if I could turn back time, I swear to you, I would have told you how I felt. We can't, and I get that. Just like I understand you walked away with a piece of me I thought I'd lost long ago. Take care of yourself, Quivina. And your beautiful soul."

Oh my God, it moved me.

Almost all of the eighty 360Project kids were at this week's Inspiration Alley event, and they looked excited to be attending. I didn't delude myself that it was easy for any of them to get to the middle of Midtown Detroit when most didn't live anywhere near there, thanks to skyrocketing housing costs near downtown. We'd given out bus tickets and some transportation vouchers to the students who had mobility issues. And there they all were. Only four students who'd had to work, as they contributed to their family's income, hadn't come. I turned around to face them in the theater and gave a big smile to the room. Proud of what my idea had become.

"Hi everyone," I said, loud enough for everyone to hear.

I could hardly see the back of the room from the lights shining on the stage, but something in the atmosphere changed. I glanced around for a second and saw familiar faces, but no sign of Max. Since it was my night, I understood that. We all had committed to hosting one of the six events. But I'd hoped I'd see Max.

"I think most of you know who I am, but for the record, I'm Quivina Adedeji, Professor of Algebra and Physics." The kids gave me a round of applause, and I tossed up a wave to all corners of the small theater. "Aw, thank you. We'll get right to it. Most people don't love math, but my brain always just naturally tried to pick apart equations or puzzles. And I'll be honest, I wasn't from a family who believed girls could, or should, go down the math route. As a Nigerian American, it was expected that I study to become a doctor until I met my husband. And while math helps in the medical field, there was one thing that kept me away. The blood." I feigned nausea and clasped at my throat.

Laughter trickled over the room.

"And then, I figured out something else. Math was freeing. But it wasn't a teacher who inspired me. It was an actual chemist from a school trip to Dow Chemical. She was a Black woman... I'd never met anyone so smart, and she looked just like me. I... I almost couldn't believe it. Her clean white coat and her dark brown skin were nearly majestic. We spent the day with her, and I learned so much about chemistry, molecular structure, the importance of negative and positive ion charges within atoms... it was invigorating. So, I read and studied and knew I wanted to be a chemist. That was until I took a physics course in the eleventh grade and I said, self... this is it. The laws on motion and propulsion kind of took over. I'd never be the same. Sometimes something comes into your life and it opens your eyes to the thing you've always wanted."

I paused for a moment, considering the words and the way they landed on the kids in the room. And then I saw him. For a moment, I was stunned. It seemed as if I hadn't seen him in decades, when it had only been a few days. All the air pulled out of the room, and I had no idea I'd started walking closer to the edge of the stage until I was already there.

The shuffling in the audience clued me in to the kids turning around to see what I was staring at. "So, yeah. It was everything I wanted in a career, and I knew if I walked away from it, I would miss something wonderful. The point of all this is, don't squander the moment you've been given. It's important to find the beauty, where you belong, and where you want to be. I didn't have this movie when I was a kid, but I did have my own hidden figure at Dow. I'll shut up now and get to the movie. *Hidden Figures* starring Taraji Henson, Octavia Spencer, and Janelle Monae. Afterwards, we'll have a discussion session, and I have handouts on the women featured in the film, along with refreshments."

I focused on the kids, giving them a smile and ensuring that they knew how important they were to me and how much had gone into the event. With another round of applause, I headed offstage and took my seat near the front, my heart hammering in my chest. I wondered, then waited, to see if Max would come to sit near me. There were reserved faculty chairs in the front of the room, but he'd been near the back of the room. I just wanted the night to be over. While I couldn't make him change his mind, I knew if there was any chance for us, I wouldn't pass up the opportunity. I did want to speak to him, but if it was his choice not to be with me... I would have to deal with it.

I spent the whole time during the movie looking for him. Was he really not going to say anything to me? His message played again and again in my mind. *Just like I know you walked away with a piece of me I thought I'd lost long ago.* I could almost see his face, his mouth, as he labored over the words.

We were into the questions before he surfaced. I caught a glimpse of him in the shadows backstage, his unmistakable frame and locs spilling over shadowy shoulders.

"Professor Adedeji, I've been thinking about majoring in math... something. I don't know what, but I love working with numbers."

The young girl, Marguerite Rosas, had a look in her eyes that reminded me of the first time I realized I could do it. "Oh wow, I think that's great. It's okay not to know which discipline. The important thing is you have some idea about what you love." I reached into my pocket and pulled out a card to hand to her. "Here, give me—"

"Oh, okay. Can I just text you my number right now?"

I had to smile at my old-school thinking. "Absolutely." She pulled out her phone while I gave her my cell number. When the text came in, I saved it under *Marguerite*. "Okay. We can meet next week," I promised.

"Thanks so much."

"You're welcome. I'll text you a few times that work. I'll try to keep it really close to the end of the day."

"Thank you. I work at night, so..."

"Completely understand. If you'll excuse me, though. I have to go talk to Professor Wynn. Do me a favor and remind everyone my door is always open."

"I will."

I returned her smile and gave her a pat on the shoulder before she turned away to head off to a group of other students. If nothing else that week had been good, at least I was actually making a difference in a young person's life.

The warmth in my chest remained as I made my way to Max. He was sitting on a bench near the stage watching as I walked up. His eyes, normally alert and daring, were half lowered with a distant expression even if he stared straight at me.

"I was wondering if you even wanted to speak to me." His voice was low and steady, the equivalent of a sexual intoxicant if there was such a thing.

I took a seat beside him and looked over. His body was rigid instead of relaxed. I could feel the tension radiating from him. He closed his eyes and leaned his head against the wall behind us. "I've been sitting here trying to work up the nerve to come see you. I couldn't do it though. So, here we are."

"I—um, talked to Smith," I said. "I had to explain... I should have been clearer with him. That I wanted you... all along."

"Wanted?"

"Yes. From the start, I felt something with you even when I was numb from all the shit that happened to me... all the bad things that went on with Kenyon, the deadening sensation of not having control over my life had taught me to never even fight. When we met and you looked at me, so annoyed I thought flames were going to come out of your mouth, I wanted to fight you. I was so angry, and it had been so long since I was pissed at anyone. It was almost... what's the word I'm looking for?"

Max still didn't look at me, just released a loud guffaw into the space. "Freeing?"

"Yes, that's exactly it. I felt free. To be angry and have emotions and do whatever I wanted to do for the first time since I was a kid. Do you know how good that feels?"

"Quivina, do you realize you're telling me I have the power to change lives just by being a pure asshole?"

"Absolutely." I giggled and placed a hand on his knee. "You were like an adrenaline shot."

"Damn, girl. You know how to compliment a guy."

"You started it. But seriously, I...I listened to your messages. They were—"

"I think I made a mistake when I told you we couldn't be together. I shouldn't have called you repeatedly when I told you I wanted space. I was confused, and I'm sorry for that. But I needed to make sure my brother understood the situation. And I misunderstood your actions."

"If there's one thing I know about you, you are one of the most caring people I've ever met. I see how you take care of your family. How you tried to take care of me, even when I was being unreasonable. I probably should have given you an opportunity to explain. I've spent my life running. I have to stick around for the hard stuff sometimes. That's the funny part. I fought to be independent and make my own choices, but every time I had to do that, I took off. I made a conscious decision to run out on the situation instead of expressing my feelings."

Max slipped his hand over mine on his knee, then followed it up with a sharp breath. "If every time you tried to stand up for yourself, you were smacked down, running... to retreat was a learned behavior. You just have to unlearn it."

Despite being at the event, I leaned over on his shoulder. I needed to feel him against me, if only for a fleeting moment. His smooth cotton shirt against my fingertips reminded me of our bodies moving against one another in the night. "It's going to take some time. And maybe a little therapy."

"I could wait for you. I can… I will wait for you."

I lifted my head to meet his eyes. "It's not fair of me to ask when there's no time period."

"I wouldn't be the one for you if I turned my back on something good, something right, just because you need time. I feel like I've been waiting for you my entire life… and I'd do it again." Max ran the back of his hand down my face. "I won't pressure you. And I don't want you to worry about whether I'll be here when you're done."

"I appreciate that… thank you. I wasn't saying I didn't want to see you, though. I just think we have to take it really slow. Like, turtle slow. I have things to sort out, but I can see… I know I want you."

"Quivina… I've never wanted anyone as much. But you've got to stop looking at me like that. There's a room full of kids on the other side of the curtain. We have to at least pretend to be role models." Max wasn't one to smile often. Not like he was smiling now, his full lips curved upward, crinkles around the corners of his eyes. It was like finding the answer to an equation or solving a riddle. Because through Max's smile, you could see his heart.

"Alright. But we have to continue this conversation later."

"Oh… is that what we're continuing later? A conversation?"

I had to laugh and fought against my need to hold on to him as I pulled away from him. The heat of him was instantly missed and I could have left with him right that moment if we didn't have young minds to shape. "Yup. I'm talking to you all night long," I teased.

Max was still holding on to my fingers as I stood, stroking the pad of his thumb over my knuckles. "I'm going to hold you to that," he said.

"As long as you're holding me, I'm good with it."

Chapter Twenty-Five

MAX

"YOU DID a great job with those kids tonight." I handed Quivina a glass of wine. We'd practically run to the cars and broken speed limits getting back to my place. I had to wonder whether we'd make it upstairs without tearing one another's clothes off. Damn. She fed my desires with every part of her, from her scent to her mouth to the graceful flow of her skirt as she walked away.

"Thank you, for both the compliment and the wine. It's been rough. You know, when I talked to Smith, he said he knew you liked me. He said when you told him about needing to work with me that night, the first night, you were weird... so..." Quivina moved her shoulders in almost a shimmy.

"He didn't tell me that."

"Well, he told me. Once he hung up on me twice. I had to catch him at the field with his players. He didn't want to make a scene, so he listened to me. We made our peace."

"And we made ours." I took the seat next to her on the

couch and tried not to watch her legs crossed in the short skirt. "He kind of gave me a blessing. After he cursed me out."

"And I thought I'd gotten the worst of it."

"Nah, he saved that for me."

"Worth it though... I mean, I enjoy being here with you. Right here."

I took the glass of wine from her delicate fingers and set it on the table next to mine. "Totally worth it. The wait and all." Using the back of my hand, I stroked down her face, a finger trailing over every smooth plane, the curve of her cheek, down to the full swell of her puckered lips. I wanted to taste her, but I wanted to do it slowly. I felt like a starving man as I looked into her eyes. "I saw you last Saturday. I should not feel like this." I stole a chaste kiss. "I should be fine. I hadn't had sex in..."

"A really long time." Her giggle shimmered into the semi-dark room.

"Yeah, well... not that long. Anyway, usually, after one time, I'm good. And we did it..." I kissed her along her collarbone after peeling back the collar of her button-down shirt.

"We did it a lot." She giggled again as her hand slid into my hair.

"So, I should still be fine. But I'm not." I opened another button on her shirt.

"Oh no, I wouldn't say you aren't fine."

"I love the way you compliment me, girl." My fingers played at the next button while I licked the shallow chasm between her breasts. Quivina shivered against me. I lowered myself onto the floor in front of her and slowly opened the rest of her shirt. Her body arched forward as if craving my touch. Her bra had a front clasp, and I could have done the happy dance. I flipped it open.

"Are you going to keep up this slow torture all night or—"

"Patience. We can do it fast another day. I want to take my time with you, if that's okay." I kissed her from the concaved area between her breasts down to her belly button. As I placed my hands on her hips, she raised her body as if to make it easier for me to slip off her panties. I followed her guidance, sliding white lacy panties that resembled shorts down her thighs. I didn't even take the time to slide them off her feet before I, practicing restraint I wasn't even aware I had, nudged up her skirt to reveal her landing strip of curly hair at her center. It was hard not to just dive into her, but I wanted her to enjoy it. Guilt-free sex, I surmised, would be so much better. I wanted to show her.

I lifted her legs over my shoulders and dragged her down just a bit, thankful for my decision to purchase the deep couch. I wanted her free to scream my name as I dipped inside her. The sharp intake of breath let me know she appreciated my efforts. I laved her clit with my tongue, dipping it in and out of her wetness. The delicate folds pressed open with my thumbs, I was able to see all of her, every delectable part, as I indulged in her.

Her orgasm was coming. I could feel it as her thighs tightened around me, but I didn't want that. Not yet. I slowed my pace, relieved some of the pressure on the tight nub, and moved downward to sink my tongue into her entry. The scent of her spurred me on, my cock rock-solid in my pants. With one hand, I opened my belt, button, and zipper, allowing the material to slide down my thighs.

"Max, I want you..." she purred as my exploration of her body continued.

Using my lips, I massaged her sex before opening wide and suckling the soft flesh. She was mine, every part of her. And as caveman as that fucking thought was, I knew I would never think any other way about Quivina. She was the one person who, despite our rocky start, made me feel alive. I'd been walking around with blinders on, my entire body shut down and restricted from all the emotions that moved life from just living to blissfully alive.

She moaned for me again, and I pressed two fingers inside her, latched onto her clit, and worked her with every skill I'd ever learned to please her.

The rise of her hips pushed her harder against my mouth, and she rocked slowly, sucking in wind as she went. I pulled my fingers from her and held on to her slowly gyrating hips before beginning the part of the ride she'd never forget.

I gingerly licked at her, then suckled, savoring her taste. Quivina bucked hard against me, her thighs trembling against my neck. I released and went in again, the same way but with more intensity than the first. A low, long groan escaped from her as she ground against me.

"Don't stop... Max, don't you fucking stop," she demanded.

It was the first time she'd demanded anything of me, and I loved it. A string of curse words came, mixed with Yoruba. I wanted to talk back to her, but I also didn't want to release her—the taste of her filled me up.

"I'm coming... oh God... it's so good... Fuck..."

I needed to hear her. I needed to breathe her in like air. She was my one person on the planet, and I resolved to give her all of me from that moment on, because the reward was so great.

Once more, I journeyed to her depths, my range of motion impaired by the yoke of her body over me, thighs squeezed inward.

"I... I'm... oh my God..." Her hands slid into my hair, and she pulled me impossibly closer to her. I loved the feel of her fingers on my flesh as she cried out in pleasure. I loved the way she rode out her orgasm on my face, and I loved being inside her—fingers, tongue, cock, everything. I took her in, milking the orgasm from her body until she was spent.

She collapsed onto the couch, her ass still in my hands, legs lagging at either side of me. I rose to my full height after gently removing her legs. "You okay?"

Quivina looked up at me as if she was stunned I was still there. Running a hand over her face, she laughed, a bark that bounced off the walls. "No, I am definitely not okay. I don't even know if I can stand after that." She licked her lips, probably parched from all the screaming.

I stared down at her, her shirt open baring her round breasts and tight nipples, her skirt around her waist, crumpled and revealing her wet sex. I wanted to take her again, but not on that fucking couch. I needed her fully naked, spread-eagle and tangled around my body. "Don't worry about walking." I leaned down and gathered her up into my arms.

"Woo," she yelped as I pulled her up, but I didn't let her get it out fully. I locked down onto her mouth with mine, tasting the wine mingled with the minty taste of her.

"Ummm…" she moaned into me as I deepened our kiss.

Her mouth on mine and our tongues dancing against one another made me harder, and I realized if I stood there with her like that much longer, I would blow. "I'm taking you to bed. I need to, Quivina." I growled the words, the vibration rattling in my chest.

"Oh, I get to see your bedroom? This is new." She waved her hands and feigned surprise.

"You haven't even seen new." I stepped out of my pants and carried her off down the hallway and to my bed. I rarely slept in there so at least it was made. Shit, I rarely slept at all, if I were being honest. Three to four hours on the couch was as much as I could take. But my old bed was about to see more action than it had in months. Maybe years. Since my divorce, I rarely brought women back to my place and no one had actually made it to my bedroom since I was married. But Quivina could have full access to everything, everywhere in my apartment. It would have been too weird to say aloud in such a new relationship, but I knew.

I lay her on the bed and kissed her before I stood to remove the rest of my clothes. I leaned over, then turned on the lamp nearest the bed to find my box of condoms.

"You are one beautiful man, Maxwell Wynn."

I stopped and self-consciously looked down at my body, which wasn't ever the traditional Morris Chestnut build, but managed to recover. I shifted to give her a light smile. "You ain't too bad yourself, girl." I continued my condom quest, grabbed one, and ripped the wrapper.

"Let me..." Quivina sat up on the bed and scooted to the side, her legs falling open over the sides. She took the half-wrapped sheath and held it between her fingertips. A drip of pre-cum formed on my tip, and she leaned forward and ran her mouth up and down my entire length. My knees felt wildly unreliable, but I grabbed the nightstand for the ounce of stability it provided as she withdrew. Elegant fingers wrapped around my shaft, and she used her other hand to skillfully roll the rubber over me. I shivered beneath her touch. Damn, she was going to be my undoing.

When she stood and unzipped the side zipper of her skirt and let it drop to the floor, I knew I'd seen glory inside her as she stood with just her shirt open, full breasts on display. I couldn't wait any more. I pulled the shirt and bra open and down her arms as I seized her mouth, using the cottony-soft material to pull her closer to me.

"I can't resist you... I could never," I whispered into her

mouth. If I'd never spoken the truth before, that was it. That I could never stay away. I was into her so much I couldn't stand it.

"Good. That was all part of my plan."

And I didn't want it any other way.

Chapter Twenty-Six

QUIVINA

I WAS CONNECTED TO HIM. I was able to tell him what I wanted, what I needed. It was liberating. And sexual attraction certainly did not equate to love, but overwhelming, all-encompassing bliss wasn't off the table. I felt him.

Between my thighs, his body rocked me in a cadence, a magical rhythm of our own. I stared down into his eyes, another first, as we melded together. Our bodies were one.

Max held on to me, his fingers sinking into the soft flesh of my hips, his large warm hands guiding my movements, the push and pull near perfectly synced.

"You feel so damn good." He closed his eyes as if the pleasure were too much to bear.

I felt like a goddess in his arms. Leaning forward, I clutched the pillows and increased my pace, desperate and greedy to drive him over the edge. I wanted to give him what he'd given me again and again. He stiffened beneath me, and

I knew I was in control. He'd given it to me freely, and I rolled my body until his grip on my flesh was like iron.

Searching out his mouth, I kissed him recklessly. Our mouths seared together as he moaned into the kiss. His erection swelled inside me, and I knew he was on the verge of losing all control.

I drank it up—his lust, his desire, the thrill of giving him all the passion I'd hidden for so many years. As he came, he bit into my lip and clenched onto me. I trembled, the feeling of acceptance the most powerful of all aphrodisiacs, and collapsed onto his chest.

"Three times tonight. I swear I won't be able to move tomorrow. I'm too old, Quivina."

"Only a year older than me." I kissed him on his chest and rolled to the side, immediately missing our connection. I snuggled into the crook of his arm and leisurely wrapped an arm around his waist.

Max kissed me on the forehead and pulled me in tight. "Yeah, tell that to my back."

"It just means you need to get more practice in."

"Just you wait. A year can make a difference on your knees."

"Yes, well... maybe we can work on this together." A red flag went up in my mind, one I wanted to press down but couldn't. I didn't know a lot about Max. I didn't know his hobbies, whether he folded his laundry or just left them in the basket... How did I feel so comfortable with a man, give him things even denied to my ex-husband, and not even know whether he liked avocado? What was his favorite color? What if it ended just like my marriage had?

"You're thinking really hard," he said. "I'm not fifteen. I'm not going to run off into the night after getting sex. I like you, probably more than I should. And I want to stick around."

"How'd you know… I was thinking about that? Well, not that, per se, but for sure how little we know of one another and the contrast to what I'm feeling?"

"I guess it's old age. We all have the same fears, Quivina. Maybe they manifest in different ways, but I'm as afraid of being hurt again as you are. In case you're wondering, vulnerability isn't one of my strong suits."

His finger ran slow designs along my shoulder. I squeezed him a little tighter. "Yeah, I'm afraid. But, in these last few weeks, I've realized I need to take control of my own destiny. And part of that is doing things I'd always been scared to do. So, if slipping down my mask to let someone I barely know peek at my soul is on the agenda, I'm going to take the chance."

"Goddamn, if I wasn't sure I'd have a coronary incident, I'd make love to you again," he said, a hearty chuckle escaping after. "I love a woman who knows who she is."

"And I adore a man who knows when he's about to have a heart attack."

"Funny girl…"

The night ran into morning with us talking about all the things we hadn't had the chance to share before. All our hopes and dreams, the ones that had crashed and burned along with those we still hoped for, everything we wanted out of life but were too afraid to reach for, and all the waiting for something to make sense. We laid ourselves bare, filleted each other down to the soul. It was truly magnificent.

The sun rose on us entangled in one another's arms, and while I hadn't slept a wink all night, I was energized.

I slapped him on his jogger-clad ass. "Those are rather skinny cut for a Gen Xer. Changing sides?"

He glanced over his shoulder as he moved bacon around in a pan. "Fashion is for any age, thank you very much."

"Senior citizens included."

"If you are forty-five, you should not be making fun of someone only a year older."

"I can make fun of anyone I want." I pulled my towel tighter around my body and poured a cup of coffee. "Think the neighborhood association will kill me if I go upstairs in just this towel?"

"No, I don't. But I don't want you walking around the building peeping toms in a towel. That ass belongs to me."

"Wow. That was pure barbarian. I didn't know you had it in you." Tossing him a humored expression, I headed to the fridge and leaned in to locate the creamer. Just as my hand was on the bottle, I felt Max press into me, his hardness evident through the cotton material of his pants.

"Whoa. Did you take a nitro tab, bud?" I closed the door and turned around to face this magnificent man. Wrapping my arms around his neck, I stood on my toes and planted a kiss on his full lips.

"You gotta stop with the elderly jokes. I'm gonna get a complex."

"Not Mr. Badass Maxwell Wynn? You would never." I kissed him again.

"You'd be surprised by the thoughts that go through my mind. And I can't have you kissing on me all the time. I still have to work today."

"Friday classes are for the birds. But you're right. I need to make some rice for my father. Baba can only barbecue."

Max stepped back and headed to the stove to remove the pot of grits and flip the bacon. "I um... I could make the macaroni and cheese for you guys."

My heart tightened in my chest, the one thing I'd held back from him. Asking him to go to my father's for support again had been on the tip of my tongue, but I didn't let it out. "You don't have to do that... I mean... I appreciate it, but… I don't want you to do anything you don't want to do or put you in an awkward—"

"I want to go. I'm just not sure I'm ready."

I had to go to the counter and grip it for support. "I don't think I have to strength to walk away from you again. You make me… I feel too good when I'm around you."

"I want to go with you, Quivina. To wherever you want me to, whenever… from now on."

I didn't dare look back at him. I just poured more creamer into my coffee because that was a real and tangible thing. Him wanting me, in the way he said it, didn't seem real. It seemed like something too good, since I'd never had anyone declare me a priority in the whole of my life. As sad as it sounded, Max's words untapped the keg of emotions I'd been holding back. I could have cried.

When his arms wrapped around my chest and he pulled me against his, I sank in. No more hiding emotions, no more sinking into the abyss of wanting to be seen yet having those prayers go unanswered.

"I'm here for you," he whispered into my ear. A warm kiss was pressed on my shoulder. "All you have to do is tell me what you want and I'll make it happen."

I grasped his forearms and nodded. "Yes. Please come with me tomorrow. I have to confront the man who taught me my needs were secondary. I don't know if I can do it on my own."

"Then I'll be there. Macaroni and cheese in hand, my hand entangled in yours."

"Fuck, you're amazing," I said.

Max turned me to face him and placed both hands on my face, then stared directly into my eyes, the soft brown of his shining as he looked at me. "No, I'm not. Not without you."

"You are disarming, aren't you?" I wrapped my arms

around him and pulled him close needing his warmth, his body to ground me.

"Yes, in fact, that's my middle name. Max Disarming Wynn. At your service."

I had to laugh again, as his hand played along my back. "Sure. Sure. But you're right. We aren't ever leaving here if we don't stop touching one another."

"I told you. You want eggs or just grits and bacon?"

"All of it. I'm going to put on some clothes since I've been forewarned about this towel in the hallways."

"I'll be here." He stepped back and landed a quick kiss, once more, on my mouth.

I couldn't help the smile that formed on my lips, and I knew I'd be smiling a lot around him. I headed out of the kitchen. Just as I made it to the middle of the living room, I heard the key turn in the lock. I froze and stared like an idiot as two children bounded into the hallway. I'd seen them before—they were the ones who'd been with Smith when he'd seen Max and me together initially. Diane and Donnie. Fuck.

"You must be Ms. Q. I'm Diane." She turned to her brother. "And this is Donnie. Uncle Smith said we'd be seeing you around."

Double fuck. "Hi... um," I glanced down at myself and quickly remembered why I should have been running. Grabbing the towel and tightening it around my thighs and chest, I closed my eyes and took a breath. "Yes. I'm... I am Ms. Q. I'm just going to go get dressed. I was, um... I spilled something on my dress and your Uncle Max was kind enough to wash it for me."

"Oh, okay. Uncle Max," Donnie called out. "We're home. And I want some grits, no bacon please."

Max came running out of the kitchen. At least he was

dressed. "Oh... I see you met Ms. Quivina. She's um... her dryer broke so... she's washing here."

"Yup. We know."

I couldn't wait for the rest of that. I bolted from the room and began throwing on my clothes. Shit, my panties... where were they?... Where? Goddammit. In the living room... on the floor by the couch.

Just as my panic hit maximum level ten, Max came in.

"Oh my God, my pan—"

He pulled the white lace from his pocket. "Are in my pants. I keep forgetting the kids' times. I'll put a board up. I'm taking them to camp today. Smith has an early practice. I should have remembered that, and I'm sorry."

I took a deep sigh of relief. "I was half-naked when they walked in. They must think we were—"

"They probably do, because kids aren't like they used to be. But I'll have a discussion with them about our relationship and explain that we're really good friends. Unless..."

"Unless what?" I took a seat on the bed and pulled my panties over my feet.

"Unless we're more than friends?"

I stopped for a moment and glanced up at him. "What?"

"Yeah, I want us to be um... exclusive. And that requires a discussion. One we haven't had."

I finished pulling up my undies before looking to him. "I think it goes without saying I won't be seeing anyone else."

"Well, I'm a little more formal than that." Max looked down at the floor, toeing a smooth swirl in the wood.

"Max. You are my man. If you want, we can get bracelets. And I think your formality is very sweet."

As he looked back up to me, his brows popped. "You are such a jokester. Come on, let's go have breakfast. We have to get moving if we aren't going to be late."

"One more thing. Can I make my jollof rice here tonight?"

"Do you know how to shred cheese?"

"You can totally buy it that way at the store, Max."

"Bite your tongue, girl. My mac and cheese is all home-made, down to the individual cheese ribbons littered throughout. The audacity."

"Calm down, Julia Child. I'll shred your cheese."

"Sounds ridiculously dirty when you say it like that. I like it."

"I bet you do." I followed him back into the dining room and sat beside Diane, who was staring at YouTube watching a gymnast do an intricate routine. "I always wanted to do gymnastics. I was too tall, I think. That's what my dad said."

"I can show you some flips if you want."

"That would be cool," I said.

Max served our grits and eggs and bacon, and we sat there, eating like a family. It was honestly the best part of our morning. I could get used to it, for sure. The warm buzz of happiness grew inside me, and I couldn't have been more elated.

Chapter Twenty-Seven

MY NERVES TINGLED beneath my skin as we made the walk up the long, low-shrub-lined walkway. Despite my efforts to keep my cool and believe it was going to be okay as Max promised, I didn't actually believe it in my heart. My course correction with Smith, opening up to who I truly wanted to be, and letting Max into my life were nowhere near as hard as dealing with my father.

Max, along with Diane and Donnie, and a steaming-hot beautiful casserole dish of mac and cheese trailed behind me.

"I'm okay," I whispered as I balanced the dish of rice in one hand. I made it to the steps and heard the footfalls behind me on the long wooden porch. I rang the bell and turned around to face the brood behind me.

Diane smiled up at me, and Donnie took in the large field next to my father's house. "Your father has a nice house, Ms. Q."

"Thank you. I grew up here."

"Oh, Uncle Max said you're Nigerian, so I thought you just moved here."

"Oh no. I moved here when I was just under your age. It's been my home almost since then."

"A long time," Diane said.

A burn rushed to my cheeks, and as Max laughed, my eyes popped up to his. "Doesn't feel good does it?" he said, a mischievous grin on his kissable lips.

"Oh, shut it," I said, the momentary giggle enough to break some of the tension.

"Quivina." The voice was unmistakable, and even as a child, I'd feared the same tone he'd used when calling my name. It meant he was pissed.

"Baba..." I turned quickly around to face him.

"Who are these people?" The condemnation in his voice was clear. And I resented him for it.

As if someone placed an iron rod in my back, I stood up, squared my shoulders, and remembered my vow to never let anyone make me shrink again. "They are my friends. And Max is my... he's, my boyfriend. Are you going to let us in? The food is hot."

As if his glare had razor blades, he cut into me with his eyes. "O mu awon agolo re wa si ile mi?"

The words, whether in Yoruba or not, sliced into my flesh. "Niece and nephew, Baba," I said, maintaining English. *Not his bastards*, I thought. My father shouldn't have said that, even if no one except me could understand him.

"Wọn ki iṣe ọmọ mi. Wọn jẹ arakunrin ọmọbinrin mi," Max said calmly. In perfect diction, he explained exactly what I had, that they were not bastards. I couldn't have loved him more in that moment. I guess in our marathon learning session, languages we spoke hadn't come up.

Fuck, did I love him?

My father, as defiant as he'd been my entire life, didn't even have the decency to look mortified. As he should have. "Come in. We are all outside."

I stepped aside. "Max, the kitchen is straight through there. If you could take our dishes in and head to the back-yard? I'll be out in a moment to introduce you to everyone."

"Whatever you need." He aimed the kids in the right direction, took my dish of rice, and leaned down, landing a solid kiss on my lips. I needed it. I needed the strength from his touch. His unwavering support.

When he was gone, I turned back to Baba. "You should not have done that... shouldn't have said that. What would my mother think of you?"

"It is not right for you to be galivanting around with such a man."

"African American? One who cares so much for his family, he deprived himself of basically having a life to take care of his brother and sister when their father died?"

"No matter—"

"Yeah, it does matter. Listen, I wanted to spare you this scene at the party. I'd hope we could sit down and talk, but you leave me no choice, Baba. I was in a horrible marriage. One with abuse, neglect, and sadness. I nearly lost the most important thing of all. Myself. And if you love Kenyon so much, maybe I shouldn't be here at all." The words came rushing out.

"He did not abuse you. You lost the babies. You had one job," he spat out.

"One job? Do you know he left me facedown in a bath-room, refusing to touch me? To comfort me at all as I bled out on the floor? You sound as if I should have died too." The thick accent of my youth came out as I ranted in my native tongue.

"If you would have taken better care of yourself instead

of doing God knows what with a lesbian in college, you would have been better prepared."

"That lesbian has been more family than you these last few weeks. You haven't even checked to see where I was living. You, Father, are intolerable. And as much as I love you, if you do not treat me with more respect, you will die alone. And that's not what I want for you."

"Um..." Someone else called from behind us. Both of us turned to find Nell and Trinity standing on the porch. "Are we interrupting something?" Compassion showed in Nell's eyes as she looked from me to my father.

"No. Welcome. Nice to finally meet you face-to-face, Trinity," I said.

Trinity's olive cheeks lit with color, but she smiled and extended a hand to me through the doorway. "Nice to meet you."

"Listen, come on in. Max and the kids are outside. Just head on through. You remember the way, Nell," I said.

"I do. And hello, Mr. Adedeji. It's really good to see you. This is my girlfriend, Trinity," Nell said, tightness in her voice.

I turned to glare at my father. Finally, he gave a tight smile. "Welcome," he mumbled, this time in English.

After a tense moment, both Nell and Trinity brushed past us. Nell gave my hand a squeeze as she passed, letting me know she was rooting for me, just as she always had.

"That wasn't so hard, was it?" I knew I was picking at a scab, but sometimes, the message had to be hard to be understood.

"Are you telling me you would choose a man who will only leave you broken, more broken than you are now, and a lesbian, over me?"

"I don't want to... oh, God, I don't want to tell you that. You are my father. I love you so very much and all I ever wanted was your approval. But it comes at too great a price. Isn't it enough to know that I am finally finding some happiness?"

"I want you to be happy, but I also want you to know who you are."

"I know. I know, now. So, I ask you… are *you* willing to lose me over a man I'm starting to care deeply for and my lesbian best friend? Because they will continue to be in my life. I'm not going back to Kenyon. He has someone, and I wish him the best. But I would never, even if he wasn't with anyone at all, go back to him and subject myself to that kind of treatment. If you expect me to, Father, then you don't love me at all."

The silence after my words stretched between us, well beyond uncomfortable and damn near unbearable.

"Quivina, I do not condone your lifestyle… and I believe in the sanctity of marriage. Divorce is… Well, I will try to be understanding. But I will never stop telling you how I feel about things."

I swiped at the tears that had started falling. I knew a lot, like the fact that my father did not want me with Max and would never be accepting of LGBTQ people, but I knew he would try. And even if he couldn't, as long as he learned to respect my wishes, maybe we could rebuild our relationship. It would most likely be tense going forward for a long time. And while that still felt unfair to me, it was better than not having him in my life at all. "I guess that's all I can ask, Baba."

"Come in, come in. You are letting my cold air out of the house," he complained. His AC was a precious commodity. I was surprised he even left the door open during our discussion. Some things would never change.

I gave him a smile and turned to go find Max, Nell, and everyone else in the backyard. As I approached, I saw such a wonderful sight... Max and Nell were giggling. Diane and Donnie were showing Trinity something on their cell phones, and Kenyon was nowhere to be found. My father had never told me if he'd declined to come. And I decided I didn't need to know. Kenyon was no longer any of my concern.

"Hey, Nell. I see you've met Max and the kids. Did you know Max speaks Yoruba?"

She looked over to me, then back to Max, and smiled. "I did not."

"Cool, neither did I." I gave Max a playful push on the shoulder.

"I can't give away all my secrets. What would I do to surprise you?"

"I guess... Next time, give a girl some warning though."

"Alright, fine. I'll email you my CV."

"How'd it go with your father?" Nell broke in. Her expression was grave, and I knew she was worried about me. My father was all the family I had left.

"Let's just say he's bent about as far as he can. We're at a truce. That's all I can ask for."

"Well, that's better than having an ambulance called, because I was sure you guys were going to jump on each other with both hands and feet," Nell said.

"No, I can take him." I laughed.

"He cool with us staying?" Max asked.

I looked up into his eyes and saw how his brows furrowed as he waited for the response. "Well, if I'm totally honest, I didn't ask. I told him what I needed. I don't think he's actually used to that. Most of the time, I would cave and just do what he said. It'll take some getting used to for both of us."

"Well, Quivina, change is good," he said.

I had to smile. The weird thing was, I'd changed more in

the last few weeks than I had in a lifetime. Change, whether forced or decided upon, was definitely good. I stood on my toes and kissed Max, right there in the middle of my father's party, with his closest friends and mine, with my heart wide open.

"We just have to open our hearts to it." I was thankful the acceptance of my decision and my life was evident in his eyes.

My father offered a nod and Max provided the same before he pulled me into his side, arm firmly around my waist as if I was his and he was mine.

And that change was one I could get used to.

THE END

Acknowledgments

Writing never gets any easier for authors. With each new book, we have to remember how to write again – and then once we do, we can only wonder whether we've done it right this time. Will readers receive it and how will this little piece of your soul survive out there on its own. To combat all those thoughts of inadequacies and fears, we have an army of friends and family who love and support us. I wouldn't be anywhere without them. And to each of you, my dear ones, those who hold my heart and peek into my soul, I love you, I thank you, and I hope you will continue to be in my life forever and always.

To my agent, editors, cover designer, marketing team, cheerleaders, critics, fans, fellow authors... may we continue to paint the world with the colors of our hearts. Thank you so much for being there.

Love forever,
Aliza

Aliza has only ever wanted to write. Throughout her professional career in healthcare, raising two children, and eating her weight in chocolate, she never deviated from her dreams of one day, adding the notch of novelist to her belt.

Author of paranormal and contemporary novels with their strong, quirky heroines in common, she continues to write the love stories of her heart.

And perhaps, still eats just a little too much chocolate.

For more by Aliza Mann, visit her website at

www.alizamannauthor.com.